TREASURE TALE

Robert Julyan

TREASURE TALE

Copyright © 2020 by Robert Julyan
SILVER MAPLE BOOKS

Printed in the United States of America
ISBN: 978-1-7349008-0-4

To the memory of Conard, old miner, beloved uncle

PROLOGUE

Eastward, across the desert sparsely vegetated with creosote bush and yucca, the Sierra del Sombre were burnished a rich gold by the setting sun. The old prospector halted his companion mule and leaned against the beast's pack bags.

He was tired, old and tired, and this journey always was long and arduous. He'd traveled mostly by night, not just to escape the searing August heat but also to throw off or render vulnerable any people who might be following him. By night the advantage was his.

But he was old now, willing to let this journey be his last. When he reached his hidden treasure he'd fill the pack bags with enough ore to allow him to live out his days in all the simple comfort he required. Funny, how people always thought having gold ore was about becoming wealthy, but it wasn't, at least not for him. Since providence had allowed gold to come his way he'd continued living as simply as he always had. No, what was precious to him, what set him apart, what comforted him on lonely nights when the cold wind blew through cracks in the walls of his isolated, primitive cabin, was the Secret. The gold could be spent, swindled away, played out, but the wonderful satisfaction of possessing the Secret was inexhaustible.

And that he'd never share with anyone.

The Sierra del Sombre held his secret fast. No one went there. In their time Apaches had kept intruders out, but the Indians were gone, or at least he was fairly sure they were. He'd heard persistent rumors that individual Indians still haunted the Sierra del Sombre, traveling by routes known only to them, keeping watch over their mountains, protecting them. That was another reason he'd been discreet in talking about his treasure. If any Indians thought a treasure was in the mountains a gold rush might ensue—and he would be killed.

But he'd never seen any Indians—or anyone else—in the Sierra del Sombre. They weren't the kind of mountains anyone would visit casually. They were remote, rugged, forbidding. Their tortuous and steep canyons and ridges discouraged travel or exploration, especially so as they made ideal ambush sites, as the Indians had known so well.

But most importantly, the mountains had nothing that anyone wanted. Their barren cliffs were hospitable only to a few desert bighorn sheep, and the lions that hunted them. No humans came here to hunt.

And while prospectors, from the earliest days of the Spaniards, had prowled the mountains they'd never found anything significant, certainly nothing that could override the dangers they faced, especially from Indians. Especially when richer, safer prospects existed elsewhere. "Damned dacite desert," he'd heard the mountains called. So the Sierra del Sombre had been overlooked.

Fools! Now some of the richest gold ore that ever existed in New Mexico was hidden in the mountains—and it was his alone.

Once, during a long winter night in his cabin, he'd drawn a crude map to his treasure, not so someone else could find it but so he could, if something happened to him in the desert or in the mountains. Heat stroke, dehydration, a rattlesnake bite—anything that could cloud his memory. He'd hidden the map in plain sight, by drawing it on the back of a worthless mining claim plat. And besides, he'd designed the map so that no one but he could decipher its signs.

Leaning against his mule he glanced behind him. In the distance, a plume of dust. Someone else might have mistaken it for a dust devil, common at this time of year, but he knew better. He'd seen the plume off and on during the day, always advancing but never closing. That they were keeping their distance until he entered the mountains told him they were more cunning than most, but it didn't matter. The Indians had known how to deal with pursuers in the Sierra del Sombre.

So did he.

CHAPTER 1

"Swirl it around, give it a good shake," said the grizzled man standing on the shore.

Tully McIntyre, one of two young men nearby, was kneeling in the Rio Grande's cold shallows. He glanced at the older man. Tipping the hubcap-sized pan into the water, he raised it and then tilted the pan to send the water swirling around the pan's bottom.

"That's it." Tony, the older man, leaned closer.

On the shore Wendy Wilson, Tully's fiancé, lifted the Nikon camera hanging about her neck and focused on the gold-panning, clicking several shots, zooming in to avoid recording the disgusting streams of tobacco juice Tony occasionally shot onto the sand. Beside her another young man, Samster Duran, stood watching as he held a leash connected to a medium-sized dog of less-than-pure breed.

"Give it a little more action," urged Tony. Tully noticed Wendy frowning. She called the man Crazy Tony. His jeans were stained and tattered, his worn flannel shirt untucked. On his feet were dirt-colored boots; on his head was a soiled ball cap reading Motherlode Blasting Caps. Tully knew that spending the day with the likes of him wasn't Wendy's idea of a romantic weekend, but this wasn't the first time she'd gone along with Tully's expeditions, even when they involved people like Crazy Tony. And he noticed that she had positioned herself upwind from him.

1

"Swirl 'er good, boy, then wash off the lighter stuff."

Tully grunted as he rotated the metal pan faster, then paused to wipe sweat from his eyebrows.

Tony cackled. "Pannin's hard work, boy, gettin' color don't come easy, it comes by the sweat of a man's brow and the ache of his back."

Tully's arms and shoulders ached. He knew Wendy would be asking herself why anyone would endure this, just for a few all-but-worthless flakes. Obviously, gold-panning hadn't made Tony rich.

"That's it, that's it," urged Tony. "Now wash the big stuff over the edge, again and again, till there's nothin' but the fine black sand in the bottom."

"I think I'm getting there." Tully sloshed water out of the pan, most of it splashing onto his pants.

"Do it a couple more times."

Tully soldiered on, releasing more water and sand back to the river.

"Got to the black sand yet?" Tony asked.

"Yes, that's all that's left."

"Well, then, young feller, let's take a look." Tully handed the pan to the older man, who dipped it in the river and swirled the water around. Then he took a large magnifying glass from his shirt pocket and peered through it into the pan.

"Hot spit! You did it. There's color in here. I told you this was a good place."

He paused to launch another tobacco stream, then handed the glass to Tully, who peered into the pan. "Is that it there, those flakes at the tail of the black sand?"

"Yep, that's them. That's the Old Quill, sure as I'm standing here." He slapped Tully on the back as he shot more tobacco juice. Tully smiled, smug that he alone knew the term's meaning. During the California Gold Rush prospectors and miners would keep their gold dust in the hollow quills of turkey vulture feathers. Lacking coins, the gold-dust-filled quills sometimes were used as currency.

Wendy shuddered.

She turned to the young man with the dog. He too was edging closer to get a closer look. They took turns peering through the magnifying lens. "Do you see anything, Samster?" Wendy asked him. Samster pointed. "I see it too. It looks just like ... gold."

"Only smaller," said Wendy.

"What do I do now?" asked Tully.

"Put it in this." Tony pulled a tiny stoppered glass vial from his trousers. "Put it all in there, even the black sand. That way you won't lose anything. Later, when you have more, you can capture it with mercury."

Ever so carefully, Tully tipped the pan to let the fines dribble into the vial. He added more water and repeated the process, then again, until not a grain of anything remained in the pan.

"You done well, boy. Now you're on your way. I told you I'd lead you to a good spot, where there was color, and sure as hell there was. Now remember our agreement."

Tully nodded, reached for his wallet, and extracted two twenties and a ten. He handed them to Tony, who stuffed them into the pocket of his jeans.

Without thanking Tully Tony continued, "Remember, there's another part of our agreement: You don't tell anyone about this sweet spot. It's just ours. The old Rio Grande keeps its secrets—and so do we."

Tully nodded solemnly as Tony turned, spat, and

strode away toward his rusted 1960s pickup. Then Tully looked at the little vial he was holding. He grinned, approached Wendy, and offered the vial. "Here, Wendy, this is for you, as a token of my love."

"Tully, that's sweet." She leaned over and kissed him. Then she peered into the vial as she rotated it in her hand. "I think I see it."

Tully frowned. "I said we'd find color here—and we did. I didn't say we'd find nuggets. There's never been anything but flour gold here, but it's real gold. I think that's kind of exciting."

"Tully, you have to admit you have an extraordinarily low excitement threshold, but I'll concede this has been fun, in a weird sort of way. We don't meet a character like Tony every day. At least I hope we don't." She leaned over and gave Tully another kiss. "Thank you for this gift, it really is sweet."

Sensing a slackening of tensions Samster joined them. Adjusting his ball cap, whose bill shaded the back of his neck already shaded by long, wavy dark-brown hair, he said, "Did you get a load of the stuff in the back of Tony's pickup? Dynamite boxes, blasting caps, drills—that's a freaking museum—or a bomb factory—on wheels, if you could separate the valuable stuff from the junk. Tully, do you think that was a real piece of ore, the big rock he had back there?"

Tully shrugged. "Beats me. I don't think even he can separate reality from the crap he makes up. But one thing's sure: he's spent a lot of time around mines and rocks."

Under her breath Wendy muttered, "A little too much time, if you ask me. Some of the rocks got stuck in his head."

4

Tully shrugged again. "There's lots of ways to live, lots of ways to live."

"Who said that?" asked Samster. "Was it some philosopher?"

"Well, yes. It was SpongeBob SquarePants."

#

Wendy couldn't sleep. Usually she had no trouble sharing a tent with Tully and his gentle snoring, but around the campfire Samster had insisted on sharing his s'mores with Howdy, Tully's dog, and now Howdy was in full flatulence. When she could stand it no longer, she wrapped a fleece robe around herself, unzipped the entrance to the tent, and crawled out. And just in time: Howdy's intestines erupted again. Any sane person would simply make the dog sleep outside, but Tully's relationship with Howdy was deep, and she didn't want Tully ever to think that loving her would compromise that relationship.

The campsite was silent, save for desultory snoring from the tent where Samster slept. She lowered herself onto the soft, cool sand and leaned against the smooth, debarked trunk of a long-dead cottonwood beached on the sand. A few yards away the Rio Grande slid silently between its banks, the yellow glow of a waning moon the only color in the darkness.

"Color." That was what Crazy Tony had called the flakes of gold in Tully's pan. And then Tully had given his precious color to her. Such acts were why she loved him.

She sighed. Yes, that was pure Tully. They were still saving to get married and waiting for him to finish his Western History dissertation at the university—and not making much progress with either—but Tully had scraped together $50 to pay Crazy Tony to show him where he could pan a few pennies worth of gold. And yes, it had been fun—she'd conceded that—but the childlike quality she'd always found so appealing in Tully frustrated her at times like this. Would he ever grow up?

She didn't look forward to her parents' questions about the weekend. She certainly didn't intend to mention Crazy Tony.

Tully had always been a romantic—and always had a good heart. They'd met in high school and become a pair. They'd stayed together through high school and their undergraduate years in college and finally through her graduation and Tully's entry into a doctoral program. When he got his degree, he'd get an academic job-and they could get married. Such a simple plan.

Yet lately she'd begun to question it. Not her love for Tully, nor his love for her. But more and more she found herself in the expanding group—her parents, his mother, his graduate adviser—growing impatient with Tully, wanting him to halt the incessant distractions and get focused. Sure, his dissertation topic didn't excite him, but so what? One couldn't expect that everything in life would be fascinating. On most days her job at the preschool was a drag, certainly not her ideal job. But, dammit, if she could compromise her dreams to accommodate other people, so could Tully. Maybe, after they were married, she could quit her job and pursue photography. And that was the time for Tully to pursue his fantasies, after his degree and finding a real job.

Besides, if his dissertation topic was uninteresting, why hadn't he insisted on one he liked? She knew the answer:

he'd simply gone along with what his graduate adviser had suggested. Tully was brilliant at following the path of least resistance and using his formidable intellectual powers to talk himself into anything.

Was she really so different?

She started as someone settled into the sand beside her. Samster.

"Hope I didn't disturb any deep trains of thought. Something in the water woke me up. Probably a muskrat slapping its tail, but I had to get up and see."

Wendy glanced at Samster leaning against the dead cottonwood. Samster Duran, scion of one of the oldest Hispanic families along the Rio Grande, and a good friend. She knew he'd been christened Samson Duran, but kids started calling him Samster, and he decided he liked that better than Samson.

Not for the first time, Wendy wished he'd find a girlfriend, though she knew finding a mate wasn't exactly Samster's highest priority. A career slacker, he was perfectly content with his life working as a part-time mechanic at a bicycle shop, hanging out with his buds and living at home with his mother and little brother.

Wendy shook her head. She'd known Samster almost as long as she'd known Tully. Samster was Tully's best friend, and Tully often depended on Samster and his motorcycle for transportation, as Tully's ancient Chevy Vega rarely was running. Samster didn't have a car, but between his bicycles and a vintage Triumph motorcycle he got around.

Unfortunately, Wendy had noticed to her dismay, he and Tully had similar career trajectories, Tully schlepping toward a doctoral degree, while Samster just schlepped.

Wendy didn't think of herself as a schlep, but in some deep way they all belonged together; that thought disturbed her.

Wendy remained silent. Samster moved to get up. "Sorry I disturbed your solitude."

"No, please, I'm happy you're here." She felt comfortable with Samster, could talk candidly with him in ways she couldn't with other people, even Tully. "I'm just a bit confused right now."

"Tully?"

"Who else?" Samster didn't answer but instead brushed sand off the soles of his bare feet. "The little vial of gold was sweet, and I don't really begrudge the $50 he paid to Tony—"

Samster faced her. "The hell you don't. I saw the look on your face when he handed over the bills."

"Okay, I did resent it then, especially as our wedding fund could have used the money, but this has been a fun weekend, and $50 isn't that much money. Adventures like this mean so much to Tully. It's just that I wish that after this trip he'll get serious about his degree. He's just drifting."

Samster gazed at the river. Finally he spoke, almost in a whisper. "Time just flows by. As the saying goes, you drown not by falling into a river but by staying submerged in it."

Wendy's eyebrows raised.

"Sorry. Sometimes profundity just up and comes out, like a belch. Actually, the best image for Tully is dog-paddling. Trying to keep afloat—and going nowhere. Of course, I don't have a lot of experience with focus and direction, but my impression of him is that he's waiting for a big adventure that will propel him forward."

"Getting married could be like that," said Wendy.

"Tully loves you, don't ever doubt that."

"I don't. It's just that … I get frustrated. As you said, time just flows by, and I don't want to wake up one day and realize my life flowed by waiting for Tully to grow up. Do you think he ever will?"

"You knew his father, a rock-romantic if ever there was one. And you know my family, my aunts and uncles and cousins living in little villages along the Rio Grande. They're all romantics. You mention lost treasure to any of them, and you'd better be prepared to spend the afternoon. Some of them trace their lineage back to Oñate. He and Coronado were the first Hispanic treasure seekers in New Mexico. Some of their descendants still go off looking for the gold Oñate couldn't find. Maybe that's why we're still here, afraid that if we leave someone else will find the treasure.

"So you're asking *me* about growing up?" He chuckled. Then more seriously he said, "I don't know. He's the same Tully I've always known. I guess that's both good and bad."

Wendy nodded. "Maybe that's one reason I love him. You can always count on him being … Tully. And maybe that's what worries me."

"I confess I don't blame you for being worried. Drifting's okay, as long as there's no waterfall ahead." And with that Samster got up. "You can send Howdy over to my tent if you want. I'll sleep with my head out the opening."

After he left Wendy just sat, watching the river, and from time to time she recalled Samster's words: "Time just flows by."

CHAPTER 2

The raspy rattle of Samster's motorcycle launched Tully out the door of his apartment. More than once Tully had observed how everything in Samster's life fit him. His motorcycle, like his tattered green T-shirt, was grungy with oil and dust, and its much-repaired engine started only sporadically.

Tully was late to the university, as usual, and lacking time to ride his bicycle he'd called Samster, who as expected had no trouble getting loose from whatever he was doing.

"Simpson," Tully barked as he climbed behind Samster, who already was releasing the clutch and pulling away from the curb. On his way back from gold-panning Tully had stopped by the history department in Simpson Hall and found in his mailbox a note from Elnora Atkins, his graduate adviser: "Let's meet Monday at 9:30. Elnora." It was not a request.

"Whassup?" Samster mumbled over his shoulder as he twisted the motorcycle's throttle.

"Gawdamned meeting. And I'm late."

"Chill, dude, it'll be okay."

That was the trouble with Samster: he didn't live on the same planet as almost everyone else, a planet with schedules and deadlines, one where meetings with one's graduate adviser didn't necessarily turn out okay.

Tully's relationship with professor Atkins had been

rocky ever since she'd agreed to be his dissertation adviser and had taken advantage of his indecisiveness to foist upon him a topic more in line with her research interests than his. She was interested in the economic history of the West, and the topic she'd urged upon him was "The Rise and Fall of the Bean Economy in the Estancia Valley in East-central New Mexico." At the time she'd made it sound significant, even interesting, but as he delved into it he realized that what he was researching was—beans. Gawdamn beans. He was going to be the western history expert on beans.

"Thanks," he shouted to Samster as he swung off the motorcycle and bounded up the stone steps of Simpson Hall, then up the wooden stairs leading to the history department on the third floor. He checked his watch: 9:35. He was late. Elnora valued punctuality, another area of difference between them.

As he approached her office he almost collided with a nattily dressed man who made a point of brushing off his expensive sport coat as if a goat had touched it. Spencer Hill, the department's chairman, Elnora's soon-to-be-ex-husband. Tully forced a smile for him. Spencer scowled in return. Not a good sign. Asshole, Tully thought.

Maneuvering around him, Tully almost skidded to a halt in front of her open door, then peered in. She was out. He entered to wait.

Elnora's office, like the best of offices, was a unique creation of its owner. Its aged oak paneling, which mirrored the wood of her desk, was all but obscured by an eclectic assortment of oddities and memorabilia. Framed historical photos of Colorado and New Mexico mining camps—Elizabethtown, Cripple Creek, Mogollon, Telluride—

as well as photos of the modern water diversion project she had studied.

Tully still was unsure how Elnora felt about that; he'd always sensed that it had been for her what beans were for him. Reinforcing the duality was a U.S. Geological Survey map of western hydrology adjacent to a framed reproduction of Bernardo Miera y Pacheco's 1776 map showing a Southwest innocent of dams and diversion projects.

On a shelf a miner's battered carbide headlamp rested beside a burnished black clay pot made by Maria Martínez of Santa Clara Pueblo. Nearby was a mottled gray and dark-gray rock of a mineral that Tully didn't recognize. He'd always meant to ask Elnora about that. Nearby on the shelf was a historical reproduction photo of Zuni Pueblo. Centered on a wall was a framed William Stone photo taken in Chaco Canyon. And everywhere shelves of books, some new, many old and long out-of-print. The office had the vague dusty smell Tully associated with the stacks of an old library.

It was the kind of office Tully foresaw for himself someday.

Tully turned as Elnora entered the room and walked to her desk, a sour look on her face. He hoped it was due to Spencer, whom she was divorcing. She wore a charcoal wool skirt and an Icelandic sweater over a light-gray turtleneck. Her salt-and-pepper dark hair was in a well-trimmed page boy. She seated herself and arranged some papers on her desk, then looked up.

"Good morning, Tully. Glad you could make it." The sarcasm was subtle but unmistakable.

"Sorry if I was late," he said, then instantly regretted it.

Five lousy minutes, and she wasn't even in her office anyway. Did it really make any damned difference? For all she knew he'd stopped to save a man's life with CPR.

"Please sit down, Tully." The "please" worried him.

As he lowered himself into the chair in front of her desk she looked directly at him. "I'm afraid I have bad news." Tully sat in silence.

"The faculty committee turned down your proposal for a graduate seminar next semester."

Tully sagged. He wasn't entirely surprised, but he was disappointed nonetheless. He raised his head and stared at her, awaiting an explanation. He wasn't going to give her the satisfaction of asking.

After a tense moment she continued, "They felt that *Examining the 'Lost Dutchman Mine as Western Metaphor'* was a little ..."

"Flaky?"

"That wasn't the word they used. They just felt it was an unnecessary digression from more substantive issues of Western History. They also were a little concerned that the proposed field trip would be a drain on department resources. And, I hate to say this, there hasn't exactly been a long line of students waiting to sign up."

"Maybe I should have proposed a bean seminar, and we could have had a field trip to a Mexican restaurant."

She skewered him with a sharp look. "That was unnecessary."

"You're right. I'm sorry."

"I know you won't believe this, but I argued for the seminar. I thought the topic was ... creative."

Tully slouched. "What did Spencer say?" Referring to her husband and department chair by his first name was an intentional slight to Elnora, and he instantly regretted it. It was insensitive to remind her of him, especially just after what likely had been an ugly encounter.

He expected Elnora to scold him, but she didn't. Instead she just looked coldly at him. "He's my problem, not yours."

"Sorry," said Tully. "I really am."

Elnora just said, "I don't think we need to get into what individual committee members said. It serves no good purpose."

She was right; Tully already knew Spencer's opinion of everything he did.

Elnora looked down and rearranged some papers on her desk, then continued. "As you know, in this age of science and technology all the humanities are under siege, charged with being frou-frou and irrelevant, and a seminar about a worn-out, highly apocryphal treasure legend just feeds those perceptions."

"But that's what much of history is—legends. The fact that no one has ever found the Lost Dutchman has nothing to do with its power over peoples' imaginations. The entire European history of New Mexico was based on the legend of a place that never existed, the golden cities of Cibola."

"I reminded the committee of that, it was in your proposal. But they felt that was a weakness of the discipline today, that Western History has spent too much time on the romantic legends—Billy the Kid, Crazy Horse, Cities of Gold, Geronimo, Wyatt Earp, outlaws, and, yes, lost treasures—and not enough time upon the events and peoples and trends that really made history in the West."

"Like beans."

She looked directly at him. "Yes, like beans. Beans

helped ancient Indians move from being hunter-gatherers to agriculturalists 3,000 years ago. The ancient Indian civilization at Chaco Canyon was built in part on beans. Beans were a staple of early Hispanic settlers, and early Anglo settlers. After 1900 whole counties depended economically on beans, towns sprang up, railroads were built, families were raised—all because of beans. Gold may have brought people to the West, but beans fed them and allowed them to stay here. That's more than can be said of these will-'o-the-wisp treasures you're so fond of."

Tully shrugged. He'd had this discussion with Elnora before—and lost. He decided to give it one last try. "The Lost Dutchman Mine is the West's most sought-after treasure. Thousands of people have looked for it."

Elnora nodded wearily. She'd heard all this. "And failed to find it," she said with a weary sigh."

Tully pressed on. "And some of the treasures were real. Nothing transformed the West like the discovery of gold in California. 'Pikes Peak or Bust' in Colorado. The Comstock Lode in Nevada was a whole mountain of silver. Even New Mexico had a few of these treasures—"

"All true," she interrupted. "But you're not interested in the mining history of the West, you're interested in the mining non-history. The phantasms. The stuff that never happened—*because it never existed.*"

"But the Lost Dutchman *might* have existed."

"You don't really believe it's anything but an empty legend, do you?"

Tully shrugged. "Yes and no. No, I don't think anyone will ever announce they've found a fabulously rich deposit and are now filling their gym bags with gold nuggets. But, yes, I do think it's more than an empty legend.

"But we'll never know, and the issue of the tale's authenticity aside, it's still just a tale, and the National Endowment for the Humanities doesn't give money to find the Lost Dutchman Mine. Academic journals and conferences aren't interested in papers on the Lost Dutchman. Foundations don't give grants to study the treasures most people doubt exist. And history departments don't build their reputations on stuff that belongs in metal-detecting magazines." She crossed her arms.

Tully was beaten, and they both knew it. The rejection of the seminar bore a clear message: get serious about real history, meaning beans.

She uncrossed her arms and leaned forward. "Look, Tully, I'm not as unsympathetic as I'm sure you think I am. Most historians are romantics at heart, that's why we're drawn to the field. And most of us have a personal interest we'd like to pursue someday. But what I've described are the realities of the field as it exists today."

Tully nodded. "I know. You're right. Okay, I'll drop the treasure stuff, at least for now and get serious ... about beans."

But as he left and trudged the down the stairs he knew he wouldn't.

#

And so did Elnora. From her office window she watched Tully as he descended the steps of Simpson Hall, shoulders slumped. She regretted not being completely candid about Spencer's role in the committee's rejection of Tully's proposal. Actually, Spencer had been the most outspoken critic, and as department chair his opinion swayed others. He disapproved intensely of Tully, something Elnora suspected was driven in part by Tully being everything he wasn't: imaginative, empathetic, genuine, and well-liked.

Students and faculty alike despised Spencer. When they got past his superficial charm, they discovered him to be arrogant, dishonest, petty, and vindictive. Not for the first time she regretted how long it had taken her to get past the superficial charm.

And Tully ... she'd hated to dash his enthusiasm, but it was for his own good. For all his flakiness—and, dammit, he *was* flaky—he also was brilliant and creative, full of life and ideas. He was just what the field needed. But everything she'd said to him was true: he had no future as an academic historian if he went astray into pastures of locoweed.

Yet she'd also spoken truly that most historians were romantics at heart. She was. When she'd entered the field she'd wanted to write about Hard Rock Molly, a semi-legendary woman in the Colorado mining camp of Ragtown. She'd wanted to learn whether Molly was real or not. But colorful stories aside, only a few scraps of hard evidence suggested she might have been, and there certainly wasn't enough there to make a decent dissertation, so she'd studied the Yampa River Water Diversion Project instead. Its economic impact on the West was enormous. It actually was more interesting than she'd expected, and her dissertation, later published as a book by a university press, made her reputation and resulted in her present job.

But sometimes she felt she'd betrayed Molly, imagined her saying, "I *was* real—but now I'm lost.

#

From beneath a pile of dirty red rags and loose papers a phone rang. A grease-stained hand picked it up. "Wobblin' Wally's Bike Shop, Wally here. Oh, hi, Elron. Yeah, he's here. Hey, Samster, Elron's on the phone."

Samster stepped from behind a bike stand that held a battered mountain bike clamped in its jaws. He wiped his hands on his shop apron and took the phone from Wally.

"Whassup, lil dude?"

"Does the bike shop have any copper wire?"

"I think so. Whassup? How much you need?"

"Three feet, thin, preferably rubber-coated. To repair a blown electrical circuit, with enough left over to strangle Richard."

"Whoa!" Normally his little brother was conspicuously even-tempered, almost to a fault; his obvious anger now was way out of character. "What's going on? What did Richard do this time?"

Richard was their mother's current boarder, the latest in a long line of hard-luck cases to whom their mother had rented a room since their father deserted the family soon after Elron was born.

Peggy Provine had a big, gullible heart, and over the years there had been no lack of people eager to take advantage of her goodwill. Most she met at the craft fairs where she sold ceramics to supplement her meager income as a receptionist at the university. Richard used Peggy's garage to make crude wooden sculptures of bears and eagles and buffalo. He had begun claiming Indian heritage and insisted his real name was Lone Elk.

"Lone Elk Richard was working in his 'studio' cranking

out some schlocky eagle when he had the bright idea that he'd get more power out of his electric chain saw if he replaced the 10-amp fuse with a 30-amp fuse. He blew out the electricity in the whole house. Now he's whining that he can't finish his eagle, oblivious to the fact that Mom's electric kiln also is down and she may have lost an entire load of glazeware. He invited his best friend, Bill Budweiser, to come over and console him."

"Have you told Mom?"

"Not yet, she's still at work. And obviously Richard hasn't bothered to tell her. That's why I was hoping I could fix things before she gets home."

"You think you can fix it?"

"I've rewired the circuitry of computers. I don't imagine a house would be more difficult. It's just a matter of logic."

Samster nodded. Actually Elron probably could rewire a nuclear power plant.

"Okay, I'll get some wire and come over. See you in a bit."

But first he needed to see his mother.

#

As receptionist for the university's honors program Peggy Provine gave a warm welcome to everyone who called or stopped by, and her greeting was no less warm and sincere when her son walked through the door.

"Why Samster, what a pleasant surprise. What brings you here?" The desk at which she sat had numerous objects on it not related to her work, including a fluted glass vase holding some hand-plucked lilac blossoms. The vase had come from a craft fair, the flowers from a vacant lot on her way to work that morning. Their fragrance suffused the office.

"I'm on my way home, and I'm taking some copper wire to Elron so he can try to undo the damage Richard did to the house's wiring this morning."

"Oh, dear. What happened? Is Richard okay?"

"Unless he got a beer can lodged in his throat since I talked to Elron."

"Oh, Samster, that was mean." She began rearranging the papers, pens, and notepads on her desk. "I'm sure it was an accident."

Usually Samster would have apologized to avoid distressing his mother, but today he simply didn't feel like it. "Mom, that guy is a disaster. He needs to go. You're lucky he didn't destroy the house, but he did manage to shut down your kiln in the midst of a firing, so you've probably lost whatever was inside."

This time a serious frown darkened Peggy's face. All the work that had gone into the load wasted. Knowing this was what moved Samster to talk to her about Richard. Maybe, just maybe, she'd get angry enough to boot him out.

She continued arranging things on her desk, then her hands found a smooth, heart-shaped stone with the word's Love and Peace painted on obverse sides. She picked it up. A bad sign. It was her worry stone. She'd traded a ceramic mug for it at a craft fair a couple of years ago. A great believer in New Age spirituality, she was convinced that rubbing the stone would channel the energy of Peace and Love.

"Mom, he's just using you. If he burned the garage down he wouldn't spend a penny on repairs or lift a finger

ROBERT JULYAN

to help fix it. He doesn't even help you at craft fairs."

"That's unfair. He would if he could. It's not his fault he has a bad back. That's why he can't find a job."

Samster shook his head. His mother had slipped into the role of being Richard's defense attorney. Now he was an underdog who needed Peggy's understanding and support. Samster's cause was lost.

"I know I'm wasting my breath, but that guy is a disaster waiting to happen—and both Elron and I know it. We don't want you to get hurt, Mom."

Peggy smiled sweetly. "That's very kind of you two. I know Richard doesn't mean any harm, but I'll be careful. Now, here, why don't you rub this stone, it will make you feel better."

CHAPTER 3

In the teachers' lounge of the Happy Jelly Bean Preschool, Wendy sagged into a purple bean-bag chair. "It isn't enough that I spend my day talking kiddie-talk, now I take a break sitting in Barney's lap." But she was too tired to move to a different-colored bean-bag chair.

What a day it had been! Diantha's mother had come in for the second time this month to insist that her six-year-old daughter be taught algebra, even though poor Diantha was having trouble mastering the concept of bodily functions numbers one and two. Then there had been Aiden, who was exploring non-traditional communication by flipping off everyone in sight. And this afternoon she'd discovered that some older boys were holding distance-pissing competitions in the bathroom. They weren't bad kids, just ... kids.

One more hour, Wendy thought, one more hour. She took a deep breath, held it, then released it slowly. A yoga teacher had insisted this exercise released stress. Maybe that was the answer, hyperventilating through the day.

She took another deep stress-relieving breath because she just remembered that after school she had to make an obligatory stop by her parents' home before finally going to her own home and her cats, her garden, and her books. Since her mother had retired from teaching five years ago she'd come to rely on Wendy for socialization, and hardly a day went by without her inventing an excuse to ask Wendy to stop by. Today it was leftover pot roast for Pip and Pippa, her cats.

But before she could savor visions of the day's end, the school's secretary entered and handed her a message. "This came while you were cleaning up the goal line in the bathroom." It was from Tully. "Can we get together in the student union later this afternoon? I need a sympathetic shoulder."

She brushed a stray lock of hair back into place. "A sympathetic shoulder, that's me." But of course, she would meet Tully and console him as best she could. After all, he'd lent her his shoulder often enough. Mutual support was among the things that made their relationship work. That, and not keeping score as to who was supporting whom.

#

Wendy found Tully, seated at the table in the southeast corner of the student union's food court that they and their friends had claimed when they were undergrads. He had a cup of coffee and the remnants of a salad in front of him. His dark green ball cap, with its Friends of the Earth logo, barely contained his long, light-brown hair, and the angle at which the bill sagged over his face conveyed discouragement.

"Hi, thanks for coming." Wendy knew that depressed voice all too well.

"I'd have been here sooner but I had to stop by the house and pick up some leftovers. The shoulder you ordered has arrived. What happened?"

"They torpedoed the proposal for the Lost Dutchman seminar."

Wendy's sympathetic frown was deepened by its insincerity. Like almost everyone else, she'd viewed the seminar as a distraction at a time when Tully needed to be focused.

Tully recounted his conversation with Elnora. "She actually had the nerve to say she'd supported the proposal."

"Maybe she did, Tully. I don't blame you for being resentful, but I don't think she's your enemy. She just wants you to graduate."

Tully sighed. "You're probably right. But that damned Spencer Hill *is* my enemy, and Elnora knows it."

"Tully, what's done is done. I understand and sympathize with your disappointment, but maybe there's good in this after all. If you do finish your dissertation, and if you get a job in a history department somewhere, then maybe you'll be able to spend time on things like the Lost Dutchman."

"The hell I will. Then the pressure to kowtow to whatever's in vogue will be even greater. Elnora herself so much as admitted that she had personal interests that she wanted to pursue but had let languish because currents in the field were flowing in other directions. And every instinct in me says that once you flow with those currents, you never return."

"Well, even if you're right, and you can't spend your time researching lost treasures, at least we can get married."

Tully's head jerked up. Never before had she been so direct voicing her frustrations. "Look, I know it's been frustrating ... but I can't get those lost treasures out of my head. I've been obsessed with them as long as I can remember. I've read every book written about the Lost Dutchman, and when a new one comes out I'll read it too. It's like a mosquito bite on my brain. When I should be studying I daydream about looking for the Lost Dutchman."

Wendy paused, looked around the lunchroom, then turning to Tully she said, "Then I think that's what you should do."

"What?"

"You—I mean you, me, and Samster—should go looking for the Lost Dutchman. It's in Arizona, right?"

"Well, yeah ... the Superstition Mountains are just east of Phoenix."

"And that's where the Lost Dutchman is supposed to be, right?"

Tully, still looking perplexed, just nodded.

"That's a one-day drive, Wendy resumed. "Spring break is coming up. The three of us should take off, drive to the Superstition Mountains and look for the Lost Dutchman. Sometimes the only way to cure an itch is to scratch it."

"But ... but we don't know where to look."

"Obviously neither does anyone else, but you must have some ideas."

"Yes, but ..."

"Then let's go. And when we come back let's take a trip to Bean Country."

#

Tully walked away from the student union shaken. Yes, he'd agreed with Wendy's plan, but it was one thing to dream about looking for lost treasures, it was another actually to look for them.

In his daydreams he always was following a promising lead or following a map–when there it was, the glint of gold, hidden from all others but him.

But while he'd spent countless hours wandering the backcountry with his father, looking at rocks, thinking he might one day find something truly unusual or valuable, he never did, nor did he really expect to.

What would happen to him if he actually went to the Superstitions and looked in earnest for Lost Dutchman? Literally thousands of seekers had been there before him– and found nothing?

But he knew Wendy was right: if he ever was to put his obsession with the Lost Dutchman to rest, he had to go look for it.

As he walked toward the university library he grew more and more depressed. And not just depressed, he realized: he was afraid.

CHAPTER 4

Tully slouched into his apartment, slammed the door behind him, and threw his book bag onto the couch, almost hitting Howdy, who was squatting illegally on the knit cotton blanket Tully had won in a raffle somewhere.

"Sorry, buddy," Tully said, "but if you hadn't been there you wouldn't have been in the line of fire." He gave Howdy a perfunctory pat on the head as the dog slunk off the couch. Hard to stay mad at Howdy, even when the dog was patently misbehaving and useless. Kind of like me, Tully observed.

After leaving Wendy at the student union and after being disappointed at not finding Samster's sympathetic shoulder at Wobbling Wally's, Tully had trudged home, stewing over his proposal's rejection and Wendy's unsettling Lost Dutchman plan. "After we've found the Lost Dutchman we'll go to Bean Country," she'd offered, as if driving around long-abandoned bean fields could approach the excitement of a trip to where a prospector with a pocket full of nuggets and his head full of images of an incredibly rich lode had fled in terror from Apaches bent on killing any White who knew the treasure's location. How could bean farming compare to that?

Unfortunately, he grudgingly knew that Wendy and Elnora and everyone else were right: the beans were real, and the nuggets almost certainly were not. He just didn't want to prove them right.

He invited Howdy onto his lap and sought consolation in the dog's adoring eyes. Then he looked around the room. Trashed, but it was good trash, *his* trash. On shelves, glittering quartz crystals, colorful agates, and scores of mystery rocks. A rusted iron ox shoe, piles of books, a DVD player, a game player, and a small-screen TV.

Atop his desk a laptop computer along with papers and pens and notebooks and more rocks. Nearby was a framed photo of him and Wendy at the state fair, standing in front of the arcade where he'd won a stuffed parrot for her. Beside that was another framed photo, of him and his father standing on a mine dump smiling and holding rocks.

On the floor piles of magazines, mostly *National Geographic*, he'd gotten free at the donation bin at the library. A soccer ball. A well-chewed tennis ball belonging to Howdy. A crocheted rag throw rug, a gift from Wendy's mom. Bowls once filled with popcorn.

On the walls, a poster of Howdy Doody, signed by Howdy himself. A dart board with several darts stuck in it. Then his room survey brought his eyes to his bookshelf. There was his copy of J. Frank Dobie's classic book of western folklore, *Apache Gold and Yaqui Silver*, about the Lost Adams Diggings and other lost mines of the Southwest.

The book had been a birthday present from his father, his father's last present before his death in an auto accident. Tully had been fourteen. He'd worshiped his father, and he loved nothing so much as when his father took him rock-hounding. He'd given Tully his own geology hammer and sample bag, and together they'd roamed wherever their fancy took them, returning home with their bags filled. Then would come more pleasant hours going through the samples, trying to identify them. His father had no formal training in geology—he was a chemistry professor at the university—but he'd trained himself, and his son, to be better-than-average mineralogists.

Inevitably, most of the rocks from each expedition would become part of the rising pile in the backyard. After his father's death, Tully would sit by himself with the rocks, examining them one by one and the memories that went with them.

His father's unexpected death had shattered Tully's world, like quartz struck by a hammer. Especially when he learned alcohol had likely been involved in the one-car accident that killed him. Tully knew his father liked to drink, but he did so quietly, alone. The drinking never interfered with his work or his family. After the accident Tully had asked his mother about his father's drinking; she would only say, "It was his only vice." Neither consolation nor exoneration.

Was that where Tully's obsession with lost treasures began? Searching the backcountry for unusual rock specimens with his father? But as long as he could remember he'd been fascinated by anything strange and mysterious. And if it had been only his father's influence he could have gone into geology and become a professional rockhound. But he knew that much as the rocks excited him, he wanted more.

More what?

He looked again at his bookshelf. A yard-wide shelf of books devoted to the Lost Dutchman Mine. It had captivated his youthful imagination; mysterious and forbidding mountains, a mine supposedly the "richest in the world," Spanish explorers, Apaches, an Indian massacre, a secretive prospector, and numerous verified but unsolved murders of searchers, shot in the head and then decapitated.

As a youth he'd read everything he could find about the Lost Dutchman and spent countless hours in his imagination following Jacob Waltz, the Dutchman, into the mountains by moonlight, pausing to look behind to ensure he wasn't being followed, wending his way through the wilderness to an obscure canyon where an outcrop of glittering gold awaited him.

No, pretty quartz crystals couldn't begin to compete with the Lost Dutchman legend.

And yet, as he'd matured Tully had realized that if ever a legend was fool's gold, it was the Lost Dutchman. Waltz never showed anyone more than a few hundred dollars worth of gold, which he'd likely stolen from a mine where he'd worked, and the man who'd found the "richest mine in the world" lived in an adobe hut in the poor section of Phoenix and died a pauper.

The credibility of the other lost mine legends wasn't much better.

Yet Tully's fascination never faltered.

So was he seeking not so much wealth as simply a legend he could believe in? A clue with some validity? A map that wasn't a fraud? He didn't really lust for gold but something far rarer: a legend, a romance, a mystery that was real.

And he resented everyone, including Wendy, who said he was just seeking fool's gold.

CHAPTER 5

As Wendy's little green Honda stopped at yet another stop light on the highway heading east, she said, "We've been driving for hours, and we haven't left Phoenix. It's been nothing but strip malls and posh residential developments. I thought Phoenix was supposed to be in the desert, but I haven't seen any desert, and I've lost count of how many golf courses we've passed. You say this is where the Dutchman lived out his final days, working a little farm here?"

"It wasn't like this a hundred and fifty years ago," said Tully. "Besides, we're not going to Phoenix, we're going to Apache Junction, which is at the western edge of the Superstition Mountains."

"I hate to tell you this," said Samster, "but a sign back there said we'd entered Apache Junction five minutes ago."

Tully looked at the shopping centers, the places hawking auto loans, tattoo parlors, and countless burger joints. This isn't what I expected at all, he thought.

He gazed ahead. A jagged line broke the flat urban monotony. "That must be them," he said, pointing.

"I knew we were getting close," said Samster, "I just saw a sign saying 'Crazy Dutchman Dan, Discount Mattresses.'"

Tully groaned. He glanced at Wendy. She refused to meet his eyes, staring blankly ahead.

Other Lost Dutchman signs appeared: Lost Dutchman Pawn and Loans, "You found it! The hidden treasure!"; The Dutchman Motel–he slept here! Free Wi-Fi; the Dutchman Diner, "Home of Golden Waffles."

Tully's depression deepened. Suddenly he pointed to a sign saying, "Lost Dutchman State Park, one mile. That's where we're headed."

"Look," said Wendy. She pointed to another sign that said, Superstition Mountain Museum. "We should go there."

And Samster pointed to a sign and said, "Prospector Pete's Superstition Mountains Outfitters, Everything you need to search for Lost Treasure. We definitely need to go there."

After more gold-seeker-themed motels and pizza joints they turned onto a well-landscaped paved drive leading to the Lost Dutchman State Park. Saguaro cacti, ocotillo, mesquite bushes, barrel cacti, teddy-bear cholla, and other desert plants flanked the road. A roadrunner ran across the road in front of them.

Towering over all were the ramparts of the western Superstition Mountains. The tawny cliffs rising hundreds of feet were pocked with grottos and hanging valleys inaccessible from below, all remote and mysterious.

"Now *this* is more like it," said Tully. "And behind this mountain are 242 square miles of wilderness. No mattress stores or pizza parlors, just wilderness not much different from when the Dutchman was here."

"Why are they called the Superstitions?" asked Wendy.

Tully happily assumed the role of expert. "They've had lots of names, mostly given by local Native Americans–Crooked Mountain, Thunder Mountain, Foam Mountains–

but the Superstition name came from farmers in the Salt River Valley, who'd heard stories of strange sounds, of mysterious deaths and disappearances, and just the general ambience of the place."

Samster stared upward. "I admit the place has a forbidding presence."

"Maybe the spirits could use a good night's sleep on a new mattress," quipped Wendy.

"Very funny," said Tully.

The parking lot of the Lost Dutchman State Park was almost full when they drove in. Patiently Tully stood in line at the reception desk while Wendy and Samster looked at the exhibits.

"Whoa!" exclaimed Samster. "I didn't know there were this many varieties of scorpions."

Wendy edged closer to look in the glass display case. "Says only one variety is really dangerous, the small, straw-colored ones that hang out under rocks and only come out at night. Well, that's reassuring. As long as we don't ever go to sleep we're safe."

Tully joined them. "Bad news. The attendant says the campground is full, has been for weeks. He said several informal campgrounds were scattered outside the wilderness area, but he couldn't recommend those."

"Scorpions?" asked Wendy.

"No, other campers. Many of them are armed, convinced people are out to steal the lost mine's secrets from them. The others are just drunk.

"He said tomorrow we could try to get a wilderness camping permit at the Forest Service office. He said our chances were slim, but we might get lucky."

"Wow, we're already treasure hunters," said Wendy, "looking for the Lost Campsite."

#

Returning to Apache Junction they found a motel, the Slim Pickin's whose logo was a prospector's pick. "We've got a couple of hours, what should be do?" asked Wendy.

"I vote for Prospector Pete's Superstition Mountain Outfitters," said Tully.

"I was thinking the Superstition Mountain Museum," said Wendy.

"Let's go to the museum and then Prospector Pete's," said Samster. "The sign said they're open until 10."

"You never know when you'll have a sudden urge to pan some gold before going to bed," said Wendy.

Tully was becoming mildly annoyed at Wendy's apparent refusal to take this seriously, but he decided not to say anything, as he usually was the one accused of inappropriate humor.

The museum occupied twelve acres off the highway leading to the state park. From the highway it looked like a Western village. At the visitor center they looked at the brochure describing the attractions. They started with the Jacob Waltz Lost Dutchman exhibit.

"He was a German, but in the Old West anyone from Germany was called a Dutchman, probably because the German word for German is *Deutsch*. He was a real person. His name was Jacob Waltz, or something like that, and you can see his grave outside Phoenix," Tully said.

"In his fifties he moved to Arizona, where he knocked around mining and prospecting. In 1870 he had a little farming homestead near Phoenix, but his farm was devastated by a flood in 1891, so he became the boarder of an acquaintance named Julia Thomas. He was in poor health and died before the year was out but not before he told her of his fabulous gold mine in the Superstition Mountains just east of Phoenix, showed her rich ore samples, and told her where the mine was. She and several others spent the rest of their lives looking for it. She also sold maps to the mine for $7."

As they wandered through the exhibit Tully continued.

"Waltz is said to have told her, 'My mine is the richest in all the world,' but he also predicted that 'No one will ever find my mine.' Stories grew that he would make periodic trips into the Superstitions and return with saddlebags filled with rich ore. People tried to follow him on these trips, but he always eluded them.

"After his death the stories grew and mutated. According to some, the mine originally was located by Miguel de Peralta around 1850, but before he and his miners could take out much gold they were killed by Apaches, who concealed it. Later an Army doctor befriended an Apache who showed him the mine's location.

"In another story Waltz had a partner in discovering the mine, a Jacob Weiser, but Waltz murdered him and kept the mine's location for himself."

Tully noticed Samster's eyes widening. "Whoa!" he said, "All you'd have to do to find the mine is look for skeletons."

Tully ignored him. "Before his death he drew a map to his mine for his landlady, Julia Thomas, then after he died of pneumonia from the flood they found a box of gold ore under his bed ..."

"Whoa!" said Samster. "That clinches it."

"Not exactly," said Tully. "The landlady and two young Germans spent several weeks in the mountains trying to locate the mine from the map and came up empty. After that Thomas began selling her story and copies of the map."

Then Samster asked, "That old Dutchman did have gold, didn't he? And it was pretty rich, wasn't it? And from what I've heard, the Superstitions are pretty rugged and remote, aren't they?"

Tully stifled another eye-roll. "First of all, those specimens he showed could have come from anywhere. Waltz worked in mines all over the West, and he could have stolen high-grade samples from a mine he worked in.

"Second, the mountains are still rugged, but they're not remote anymore. They're right on the edge of greater Phoenix, and each year hundreds of thousands of people crawl all over these mountains hiking, camping, birdwatching, climbing, and all of them keeping their eyes out for the Lost Dutchman. They've been doing that for over a hundred years—and no one has found anything."

"Third, geologists say the volcanic rocks of the Superstitions are an unlikely place to look for gold, and no other gold deposits have been found there.

"And finally, to return to my point, isn't it suspicious that 'the richest gold mine in the world' centers on a man who according to all contemporary accounts lived and died in poverty?"

Samster looked frustrated. Yeah, but ..."

"I know, I know, it's a powerful legend, but you'd be money ahead believing in the tooth fairy."

In the exhibit they paused by some rocks, with cryptic

symbols and carvings supposedly found as clues to the mine.

"This is bullshit," said Wendy. "That horse drawing looks like what I did during my horse phase in sixth grade. And besides, why would anyone who knew the location of this fabulous mine create undecipherable clues for someone else to follow?"

"She's got a point," said Samster.

They looked at the other exhibits, one of which mentioned that gold had indeed been found in the area, at Goldfields outside the mountains, but few people believed this was the source of the Dutchman's gold.

They next visited the 20-stamp mill and an *arrastre*, modern and ancient means of extracting gold from ore. Neither were original to the location but nonetheless were authentic.

Then they visited a miniature gold mine, a labyrinth, an 1890's power drill, a nature trail, and a replica of a miner's cabin.

"And now," said Samster, "something I know you'll both be interested in: the Elvis Chapel, where they perform weddings."

The scorn on Wendy's face would have withered most people, but Samster was used to it. "If we wanted Elvis for our wedding," she said, "we'd go to Las Vegas and hire an impersonator."

"It's not as cheesy as it sounds," said Tully. "The Elvis Chapel is a 1969 movie prop built for the Elvis western *Charro!*, the only movie Elvis made in which he did not sing, but played a strictly dramatic role."

"Still ..." Wendy huffed.

As they left the museum Wendy said, "I have to admit

that was pretty interesting, but I didn't see anything to convince me the Lost Dutchman is real."

"That's not the point," said Tully. "Disneyland doesn't expect visitors to go away believing in Tinkerbell."

#

Prospector Pete's Superstition Mountain Outfitters was a sprawling, awkward one-story painted cinder-block building dominated by an animated neon sign showing an old prospector swinging a pick. It blinked. Though it was past dinner time, the parking lot was almost full, with everything from pickups to Jeeps to old sedans like Wendy's to Lexuses. They walked through the automatic doors and selected a shopping cart.

"This is *not* what I expected," said Tully.

"It's *exactly* what I expected," said Wendy. Tully shot her a disapproving glance.

"Tully, let's check out the Hardware," said Samster nodding to a large sign.

"I think I'll go for the maps," said Wendy, pointing to a sign saying Maps and Books.

"Where do they rent mules?" asked Samster. "Can't be a prospector without a mule." Tully ignored him.

Hardware was the store's largest section and was subdivided into Digging Implements, Gold Pans and Washing Devices, Engines and Pumps and Suctions, Buckets, Wave Mats, Dry Washers, Sluices, Magnifiers, Picks and Shovels, Vials and Tweezers, Metal Detectors.

They ambled by the metal detectors that looked like ungainly grasshoppers, only with wires. Their prices started at several hundred dollars then went up steeply into the thousands. "What brand do you think the Dutchman used?" asked Samster.

"Okay, you're getting as bad as Wendy."

An upper-middle-aged man in denims and a flannel shirt hanging over his ample stomach sidled up to them. His name tag read Dwayne. "Y'all finding everything all right?"

"We're going into the Superstitions tomorrow," said Samster.

Tully could tell Dwayne was making a supreme effort not to roll his eyes.

"Actually," said Tully, "we'll probably prospect somewhere else"—Samster gave him an astonished look—"but as long as we're here ..."

"Sure, sure," Dwayne said.

Tully read his mind. "What the minimum we'll need?" he asked.

The man sighed. "Well, a good book on mineral identification would help, unless you're geologists, that is."

Tully drew himself up. "I've been an amateur geologist for a long time."

"Well, in that case, you'll need a good map and a couple of small bags to carry samples. They're over there, by that pretty young woman." Tully didn't know whether to be flattered or offended.

"Picks and shovels?" asked Samster.

"Forest Service won't let you into the mountains with picks and shovels, no prospecting allowed."

"But what if we find something?" asked Samster.

"I'll tell you what," Dwayne drawled with slow sarcasm, "if you find some gold, come back here and I'll dig it out for you with my teeth."

"That wasn't very encouraging," said Samster when they rendezvoused back at the car. "How'd you do, Wendy?"

"Got postcards for all my friends–and a T-shirt that says, 'My fiancé found the Lost Dutchman Mine, and all I got was this lousy T-shirt.'"

#

They arose early the next morning and after breakfast at the Waffles of Gold Diner, they drove to the Forest Service office. Despite being a weekday, the parking lot was full, including a bus labeled Tucson Girl Scout Troop 19. After a long wait in line at the counter, they finally asked the young woman in the Forest Service uniform for a camping permit.

"What month would you want?"

"Well ... we were thinking tonight," answered Tully.

The woman rolled her eyes so hard her hat almost fell off. "The Superstition Wilderness is so popular that we have to issue camping permits months in advance. Sorry."

From a room behind the counter a woman's voice said, "Actually, a party that was booked for Hackberry Flat canceled just now, and we don't have time to contact the next on the waiting list. You might be in luck."

Tully filled out the form thrust in front of him. She eyed their backpacks suspiciously. "You don't have any picks or shovels or other prospecting gear in there, do you?"

"Just some little bags to carry ore samples," said Samster.

The ranger rolled her eyes even harder. "Just so you know, prospecting and mining are prohibited in the wilderness. I suspect you're looking for the Lost Dutchman, but if every treasure-seeker dug a hole, the mountains would be just one big pit. You can look at rocks to your heart's content, but don't remove anything.

"And I need to warn you about some of the dangers back there."

"Like tarantulas and scorpions?" said Samster.

"Yeah, them, but mostly other treasure-seekers. Some of them are mentally unbalanced—and they're usually armed. All the famous deaths in the Superstitions have been at the hands of other humans. But we haven't had any incidents lately."

Wanting to change the subject, Tully said, "Looks like mild weather—can we just spread our sleeping bags on the ground?"

"Wouldn't recommend it. Rattlesnakes and scorpions are nocturnal. Be sure to check your clothing and shoes before putting them on."

As they walked out Wendy said, "How did John Muir put it? 'Let nature's peace flow through you as sunlight through the trees'? I'll bet he didn't have to worry about crazy prospectors with guns."

#

They signed the register at the trailhead, noting that visitors had come from throughout the U.S. and even Canada. "Word of the Lost Dutchman gets around," said Samster. "How many people a year come looking for it?"

"Thousands. And it's been over a hundred years that people have been looking for it—and no one's found it."

"If I dropped a rare penny here, someone would have found it," said Wendy.

"Remember what the Dutchman said," Tully said, 'No one will find my mine.'"

Wendy humphed her reply.

They hoisted their packs and walked down a wide, well-traveled trail, with signs saying their campsite was six miles away. In the distance was the stark volcanic plug known as Weavers Needle. The Dutchman said he could see Weavers Needle from his mine, but then, Tully reflected, Weavers Needle was visible from almost everywhere in the mountains. And the Needle was basalt, Tully reminded himself, and it and all the rocks there came from an ancient volcanic eruption, creating rocks notorious for lacking mineralization.

Despite the obvious evidence of previous travelers, Tully looked around at the tawny cliffs, looming over him, their clefts and grottoes hidden by dark shadows. Tier upon tier the cliffs rose, ledges connecting ledges, or ending in more cliffs. Though improbable, up there one of those grottoes might have a sub-grotto where the Dutchman's mine might be hidden.

The scene worked its magic on Tully's imagination. I'm here, he thought, finally here. And it's bigger, more complex, wilder than I'd imagined. Among those crags a person could disappear, not be found. He imagined the Dutchman walking down this trail by moonlight, long before the Forest Service or the Girl Scouts, carrying a rifle, always looking for someone following him, looking at shadows, until finally when he felt he was safe he struck off on a route known only to him, following an inconspicuous canyon, looking for subtle landmarks, until high in the mountains he came to a narrow winding ledge that led him to another ledge, narrower and steeper that ended in a sheer drop-off of several hundred feet.

Carefully he lowered himself over the edge to a tinier ledge fronting a crevice. He climbed into it until it opened up into a hidden chamber, invisible from below, and there, there was his gold deposit. It wasn't large, it had no spoils pile, just big chunks of raw gold.

This was how Tully imagined the Dutchman's mine during the long nights spent reading the books. "No one will find my mine."

And now he was here, perhaps walking in the Dutchman's footsteps. Looking at the looming, forbidding mountains, he felt the mystery still alive in him.

The path led them to a large clearing near Hackberry Spring. Nestled among the rocks and shrubs around the clearing were the bright colors of other campers' tents. Two horses were tethered near an old corral. "Over there," said Tully, "is a site with some seclusion."

"I can see why," said Wendy, as they began setting up their tents. Surrounding the site were cacti and agaves and ocotillo. "Even plants don't want us here."

After setting up they visited the spring, not for drinking water, as the Forest Service had made clear none of the water in the wilderness was potable, but rather just to explore.

"I'll bet the Dutchman drank from this spring," said Tully.

"And I'll bet he had diarrhea right where we're camped," said Wendy.

"Okay, that's enough," said Tully. "Some people took this seriously enough that they died looking for his mine."

The setting sun was turning the cliffs golden when they returned to camp. They'd explored several canyons, and Wendy had photographed the stark rock formations and several interesting plants—barrel cactus, hedgehog cactus, teddy bear cholla, century plant—but Tully said the canyons were too obvious for the Dutchman's gold; he still clung to the image of the hidden crevice high on the ledge.

Tully set up the little alcohol stove while Samster broke out graham crackers, marshmallows, the chocolate bars. "I refuse to camp without s'mores."

Wendy cooked a large pot of mac 'n cheese, while Samster boiled water for tea in a smaller cook set. After dinner and s'mores, they leaned back and told Superstition Mountain stories.

"Imagine what it would be like camping here, alone, as Adolph Ruth was, not knowing that in the dark was someone who would kill him."

"Stop," said Wendy, "that creeps me out. And who was Adolph Ruth?"

"In the 1930s an elderly treasure hunter named Adolph Ruth and his son obtained a supposed map to the mine. He went into the Superstitions alone to find the mine and didn't return. Later Ruth's skull was found—with a bullet hole in it. Then a page from Ruth's notebook was found on which he'd written in pencil, *Veni, Vidi, Vici*, Julius Caesar's phrase meaning 'I came, I saw, I conquered.'

"Since then at least four others have gone missing looking for the Lost Dutchman. Sometimes their bodies were found."

"And there have been other mysterious deaths, right?" said Samster.

"There have," said Tully.

46

"And the ranger said to be wary of crazy people with guns running around the mountains," said Samster.

"Okay, that's enough, you two."

Suddenly Samster said, "I hear something."

"I said that's enough."

"No, I'm serious," Samster said.

"I think I hear it too," said Tully.

Wendy's eyes went wide, and she strained to listen. "I hear it too. It's coming from over there."

"We should investigate," said Samster.

"Are you crazy?"

"Come on, we'll just go close enough to make out words."

As silently as possible, they crept toward the sound.

"It's singing—and I know that song," said Wendy.

"Yes?" said Tully and Samster together.

"Listen carefully."

They strained, then a breeze brought the tune closer.

> *"Nobody likes me, everybody hates me,*
> *Guess I'll go eat worms.*
> *Big fat juicy ones*
> *Eensie weensy squeensy ones*
> *See how they wiggle and squirm!"*

"Wha ... what?" said Tully.

"It's a Girl Scout campfire song," said Wendy. It's the Girl Scouts from the bus we saw."

Wendy and Samster laughed. Tully just scowled.

#

The next day, after an oatmeal and instant coffee breakfast, they set off exploring again. This time, at Tully's urging, they went up a draw with no trail. They scrambled over boulders and through cactus groves until they were at the base of a high cliff. Above, Tully could see a ledge. "I want to go there," he said.

Wendy shook her head, but Samster said, "I'll go with you."

With Wendy looking on, frowning, the two scrambled up. A chute of debris led to the ledge, two feet wide. Carefully they followed it.

At one point they had to step over a three-foot gap. Looking down they saw Wendy far below, waving her hands signaling no. They ignored her and leaped the gap. The ledge continued. When they turned the corner and it looked like the ledge might stop, Samster exclaimed. "I see metal."

As quickly as they dared they moved forward until they stood before a slender crack—with a bolt and carabiner in it. Looking up they could see others.

"Looks like this is the end of the line," said Samster, "unless you brought a rope."

"Gawdammed climbers," muttered Tully. He'd forgotten that they would have explored every cliff and ledge and crack in the mountains. Bitterly he said, "Let's get back to Wendy."

They spent the rest of the morning exploring obscure little draws and ridges, peering into rock overhangs, but Tully's heart wasn't in it. Every place they went, Tully knew, had been explored by dozens, perhaps hundreds, of people before them.

Wendy, however, grew excited, discovering new plants to photograph, new perspectives from which to photograph the cliffs.

"Hey, you two, climb up there and make like you're dangling over. That would be dramatic."

"Not now," muttered Tully.

She looked at him with bewilderment and concern.

#

Tully was sullen as they drove back to Albuquerque. "Look," said Wendy, "I knew the prospecting was a bust, but did we *really* expect to find the Lost Dutchman in one day of wandering around. It was a fun adventure."

Tully just nodded.

Tully's funk also concerned Samster. "You didn't ever really believe in the Lost Dutchman, did you?"

"I never said I believed in it. I knew the improbabilities and contradictions better than anyone. I just didn't expect it to be so commercialized and hokey. I wanted some mystery, not Prospector Pete and the Elvis Chapel and eating worms. And the carabiner."

"I'm sorry," said Wendy. "I truly am."

"All I've ever wanted was a mystery I could believe in, and now I know the Lost Dutchman doesn't make the grade. You have no idea how many hours I wasted reading about the legend and imagining the Dutchman sneaking off to his fabulous treasure. It's worse than learning there's no Santa Claus."

"What?!" exclaimed Samster. "There's no Santa Claus?"

"Very funny," said Wendy.

"I'm sorry," said Samster.

"Tully, there are real mysteries out there," said Wendy. "They just haven't been discovered as mysteries. That's where your genius and creativity come in."

"You're right. I know you're right." As they drove Wendy heard him mutter, "Back to the gawdammed beans."

CHAPTER 6

Following Tully's directions, Wendy steered her little Honda off Interstate-40 onto a smaller paved road that as far as she could see was empty of cars. Eastern New Mexico, empty country.

"Quite a bit different from Phoenix," she remarked. Tully just grunted. Since returning from their Lost Dutchman expedition Tully had been sullen, withdrawn. He was taking the disappointment hard, but he was keeping his word to go to Bean Country when they returned from Arizona, but this country could hardly be more different from Phoenix and the Superstition Mountains. Flat, unpopulated. Few tourists who visited only the Rio Grande Valley knew just how uninhabited most of New Mexico was. And judging from the population statistics she'd seen it was getting even emptier as small towns died and farmers and ranchers struggled.

Wendy watched as Tully surveyed the landscape, saw him shake his head. "Bean country. Look at this God-forsaken land. It can barely support one raw-boned cow with a couple of hundred acres. And to think that people came out here expecting to be farmers."

"Was it always like this?"

"Yes and no. It's been overgrazed, so it didn't always look as scroungy as this. And I admit that the homesteaders arrived during a wet period in the climatic cycle. But yes, arid wasteland is the default setting for this region. Look over there."

He pointed toward a weathered wooden house, long abandoned, its doors and windows open to the elements. In front were the skeletons of several elm trees; one still lived, struggling to put out green leaves.

Nearby the blades of a windmill dangled and clanged in the breeze, too broken and disoriented to decide where to turn. A dead cottonwood, surrounded by broken branches, gave testimony that no water had been pumped in a long time.

Tully shook his head. "Sad, just sad. Gawdammed beans!"

Wendy said nothing.

They drove toward the village of Pleasant Valley. They saw several other abandoned homesteads. Those made of adobe were dissolving back into the earth. Those of wood would take longer to disappear.

They passed three mobile homes that appeared to be inhabited, to judge from the pickups parked outside, but they had no active barns or corrals. Once, far in the distance, they saw an isolated stand of green trees. A dirt road led toward it beneath a sign that read Wilson-Ovitt Ranch. At the village, a sign read Pleasant Valley. Elevation 6377 feet.

"Interesting," observed Tully, "how some towns put their population on their sign, while others put their elevation. I guess that when you don't have population you always have elevation."

"It looks like there are a few people here, a few houses." Wendy slowed as the highway became Pleasant Valley's main street—completely devoid of vehicles.

"Look closer."

Wendy did. The town had houses, but no one lived in them, almost all were abandoned: windows boarded up, tumbleweeds piled against walls, paint peeling, adobe melting. Deserted.

"There's one that looks inhabited." She pointed to a mobile home with several pickups and cars parked in front of it. "And there's another." On a clothes line laundry flapped in the breeze. "There are a few people here." But she also noticed that except for a few residences, Pleasant Valley had nothing else betokening a living town: the school building was as decrepit and forlorn as the other abandoned buildings, so were the church and the store.

On the main street, a gas station stood empty behind pumps that hadn't pumped since gas was twenty-five cents a gallon and an attendant washed windshields. Pleasant Valley was more a cemetery than a town.

Wendy's initial high spirits were deflating. She wanted to go home. Given Tully's sour mood, this had all the makings of a bummer.

Oddly, Tully perked up. "Pleasant Valley may not have a preschool"—Wendy shot him a dark look—"but it does have a senior center. Let's stop."

Wendy parked the car in front of a gray-concrete building where a sign read Pleasant Valley Senior Center. It differed from the town's other buildings only in that its door, windows, and roof were intact. Beside the door was a bulletin board with several paper notices tacked to it.

"Let's see what's happening in Pleasant Valley these days," he said as he climbed out of the car, clearly enjoying sarcasm at Pleasant Valley's expense. "Yep, Pleasant Valley —neither pleasant, nor a valley."

As Wendy joined him she looked around lest someone

might be offended by his remarks, but the town didn't even have stray dogs.

"Here's a notice of a county commission meeting," Tully read. "And here's a zoning hearing notice, must have something to do with the new international airport they're putting in. Wait, now this is interesting. Someone's giving away free puppies. I wonder if they count dogs in the population figures. A couple litters of puppies could double the town's population."

Wendy frowned. Usually she enjoyed Tully's irreverent humor but not this bitter sarcasm. Maybe she could change the subject. "Here's the schedule for the senior center."

"Looks like we missed the free breakfast, but wait, there's going to be bingo later today. Maybe we can sit in, win some cutesy crafts."

"I think it could be a good opportunity to talk to some local people."

"Maybe we'll be lucky, maybe both of them will be here."

#

Wendy was silent as they left Pleasant Valley to retrace their route. She'd told Tully that she wanted to take photos of the abandoned homestead they'd seen.

"Why not?" he replied. "Maybe we'll find a dead cow, and you can photograph that too."

Wendy remained silent. She was fed up with Tully's negativity and sarcasm, but she didn't feel like getting into a fight over it. At least not yet.

At the homestead, Wendy took several minutes to assemble her tripod, cameras, lenses, light meters, and other gear. She handed the tripod to Tully.

He put it over his shoulder. "Be sure to take your fastest lens. You don't want all the action here to just be a blur."

Her lips tightened. A few more cracks like that, and she might welcome a good fight.

The wind had picked up since morning. Dust sifted around their shoes. The windmill's blades creaked and groaned as they struggled to turn. A loose shingle on the house's roof slapped its neighbors. From across the empty field a vagrant tumbleweed rolled in to join others piled against the building's windward side. In the dust around the house were the hoof prints and droppings of cows, while holes at the house's base showed that pack rats had burrowed beneath. "At least this is still home to someone."

Tully entered the house's open door, but Wendy decided to photograph the windmill first. She walked around it, seeking the best angle. She set up her tripod and camera so the windmill's manufacturer—Aeromotor—was visible. She wondered if the company was still in business. Did any farms or ranches still use windmills? She hoped she'd be able to capture the feel of a bygone era, the desolation of hopes gone bust that the windmill represented. She wondered if the windmill's pipe still reached underground water. Probably not, judging from the dead cottonwood.

"Hey, Wendy, come here," Tully called from the house's doorway.

She followed him into the house. The room had the dry, dusty smell of an attic long unvisited. "Look at this." Pages from newspapers and magazines had been stuffed into the space between the interior and exterior walls. "They were using these as insulation."

He pulled some out and spread them onto the three-legged table in the room. The Battle of the Bulge were the headlines. Carefully she refolded the newspaper and placed it on the wall, then set up her tripod and photographed it. News from World War II staring from the decaying walls of a long-abandoned homestead would make a powerful image.

Tully was excited. "Wow! This is like a time capsule. Think of living here and reading about the war in Europe. And look here." He opened a magazine. It dealt with farming. The advertisements showed shiny new tractors and combines, animal feeding systems, new varieties of seeds. One ad touted a recently developed bean variety.

Wendy handed it to Tully. "Imagine living here and reading this as your crops were failing and you were faced with leaving farming."

Tully shook his head, said nothing.

They continued exploring the abandoned house's three rooms: living room, bedroom, and kitchen. In the bedroom Wendy found the remains of a children's book, *The Three Little Peppers and How They Grew*. Kids had been here, perhaps their parents had read this book to them. What had their lives been like? Where were they now? Did they remember this place? Did they ever return?

A profound sadness swept over Wendy. "I'm going back outside, to the windmill."

They stayed at the homestead longer than they'd expected, long after Tully had begun to get impatient. She composed her photos carefully, not just for artistic effect but also out of a vaguely felt obligation, almost moral, to preserve whatever fragments of life, of memories, remained in this place.

As she put her equipment in her car's trunk, Tully quipped, "I hate to think how long it would take you to photograph a house that people still lived in."

A withering glance. "Not now, Tully."

He shut up.

#

A half-dozen cars were parked outside the senior center when Wendy and Tully drove up. They entered together. Conversation ceased, ten gray heads turned toward them, ten pairs of eyes stared at them.

Tully flashed a broad, toothy smile. "Hi, there. My name's Tully, this is my fiancée, Wendy. We don't mean to intrude, but I'm a history student at the university, and I'm researching this area's history, especially bean farming. I thought I'd get better information talking to actual people than just looking up stuff in books."

Wendy smiled too. Tully was good; if anyone could charm a bunch of old people, it was Tully.

A heavy-set woman with graying hair who didn't look old enough to be a senior stood from her place at a table at which several bingo cards were placed.

"Well come on in. I don't know as we can give you the information you're after, but if it's talk you want, we've got plenty of that." That elicited several chuckles around the tables.

"Here, pull up a couple of chairs. Elmer, get these folks cards so they can play too. Then we'll talk while we play."

Almost before they knew it Tully and Wendy were seated behind four bingo cards each and a pile of beans, pinto beans.

"My name's Grace," said the one-woman welcoming committee. She then went around the room and introduced everyone else. There were a few more women than men, and their ages ranged from early elderly to antediluvian.

"Vera, call out the numbers that already have turned up." A woman who sat behind a round wire cage called out "B-6, N-32 ..." Tully and Wendy plopped beans on any cards containing those numbers.

"Okay, I think they're caught up. You two want some coffee before we continue?"

"Actually, a cup would taste good about now," Tully said. "Wendy?" She nodded.

One of the early-elderly women filled two cups from a large urn in the corner.

"Okay, Vera, let's get going again."

The woman spun the cage, and out rolled a ball. "G-47."

"I've got it!!" Wendy blurted before she could catch herself. Around the room people said, "Me too." "Hot damn." "Just two more, Vera, just two more."

Before she knew it, Wendy was so caught up in the game that she forgot she was a stranger there. She glanced at Tully. He was hunkered over his cards.

"Bingo!" crowed a man with white, bushy eyebrows.

"Damn," Wendy heard Tully mutter, "I needed just one number three different ways."

"That's twice tonight Henry's won," someone said. "I think he's in cahoots with Vera, giving her kickbacks."

While Vera gathered up the balls and put them back in the cage, Grace turned to Tully. "Now what's this research you're doing?"

Three hours later, the bingo tournament broke up.

During lulls in the action, if it could be called that, Tully tried asking questions eliciting information about the area's bean-farming history.

Many players said they'd been born and raised in the area, working in the bean fields as children. "Those were hard times, but sometimes good times," said an ancient woman whose skin resembled that of a withered bean. "I remember when a good crop would come in Dad would take us all up to Moriarty or maybe into Albuquerque and we'd go to a restaurant and could order anything we wanted. Oh, those milk shakes! But when the crop didn't come in, we ate ... beans."

Henry Holland, who was having a streak of luck, said, "Bean farming wasn't much different from this game here. It was all the luck of the draw. But then the weather turned drier, and good years became fewer and fewer. Our family had a lot of good friends here, and we'd get together weekends after church and play cards and talk. I'll never forget how sad it was when one by one they pulled up stakes and moved on. We didn't keep in touch with any of them. My dad ran a grocery store here, and at one time we knew everyone in the Estancia Valley, but when folks couldn't buy groceries he went bust. We kept going when he got a job driving truck out of Moriarty. We lived there for quite a while.

"Now there's not many of us left who remember the old days. You should talk to Wilbur Frost. He's one of the last bean farmers who still lives on the old homestead. I'll give you directions."

Then Vera spun the wheel, and the game resumed.

#

Wendy and Tully were among the last to leave. Wendy carried a bag of pinto beans she had won, as well as a weather vane in the shape of a flying duck, while Tully also had a bag of beans, a knitted pot holder, and a *Pleasant Valley Bicentennial Cook Book*. Tully had had a winning streak.

After they said goodbye to everyone, using first names, Tully turned to Grace. "I cannot thank you—and everyone—enough for your hospitality and help. If I ever finish my dissertation"—Wendy winced—"you all will be mentioned in it."

"We're glad we could help. Not many people show any interest in Pleasant Valley these days, and we're glad to have visitors. Of course, you're not strangers anymore, so you're welcome anytime."

Tully hesitated. "I have one more question, if I may. The name, Pleasant Valley. I'm not going to say the town isn't pleasant, but it sure isn't in a valley."

Grace chuckled. "It's been a while since anyone noticed that. Actually, it's easy to explain. A lot of the early homesteaders here were from Kansas, and they brought that name from a Pleasant Valley back there."

As Wendy and Tully turned toward their car, Grace called out, "Be sure to visit Wilbur Frost, out near Cholla Flats. He knows more about the bean era than all of us put together. He lived it. Be sure to ask him about Oscar Bollinger, it was the closest we had to a mystery around here."

#

The next morning found Wendy driving down a dirt road, while Tully navigated using hand-scrawled directions

Henry Holland had given them the night before. "After the next left it should be half a mile, at the end of the road."

"Wilbur doesn't have many neighbors." Wendy hadn't seen another house in miles.

"As they said last night, he likes it that way."

Wendy turned to Tully. "Speaking of last night, I can't remember when I had so much fun."

Tully smiled. "Who'd have thought we'd have such a great time playing bingo with a bunch of old folks in the Pleasant Valley Senior Center? I think Samster would understand."

"What are you going to do with your beans?"

"Why, cook them, of course. There's an old iron Dutch oven somewhere around Mom's house, and this cookbook's got lots of great recipes. I'll cook up a bunch and invite everyone over."

"I'll come, but on one condition."

Tully looked confused. "You don't like beans?"

"That's not it. You have to promise you won't give any beans to Howdy. I live down wind from you."

#

Dogs! Wendy thought as she parked her car. Four dogs of varied shapes, sizes, and colors, all barking, burst from a ramshackle collection of weathered wooden buildings centered on a house not much larger or in better condition than the homesteader shack they'd seen yesterday.

An old man leaning on a cane appeared in the house's doorway. "Shut up, gawdammit! Just shut the hell up." He waved his cane at the dogs, who slunk back into the debris. Turning to Wendy and Tully the man said, "It's okay, they won't bother you. They're just doing their duty. Now they're at ease. Come on in."

He appeared to be expecting them. Wendy wondered how he knew, as she'd seen no telephone lines.

"Henry Holland stopped this morning and said you folks might be coming by." He led them into the main room of the tiny house. Wendy caught the scent of wood smoke mingled with that of fresh coffee.

"Henry said you have a liking for coffee." He went to the kitchen area, not quite a room, and poured two cups from an enamel pot simmering on an old propane stove. "Here, the sugar and cream are on the table." He motioned toward chairs around a table that only differed from the one in the abandoned cabin in having four legs instead of three.

A cot neatly made was against one wall, while against another was an easy chair with an oil lamp on one side and a well-stocked bookcase on the other. Through an open door Wendy could see a larger bed, also made. A small wooden building near the main building was the outhouse. In the kitchen area a hand pump was perched above a sink, while cupboards held supplies and foodstuffs. Yes, old Wilbur Frost had indeed lived the homesteader era. In fact, he was still in it.

Tully sipped his coffee. "Thank you. This is good. I hope you don't mind us barging in like this ..."

"Not at all. Even the dogs benefit from stimulation once in a while. Henry tells me you're researching the bean-farming era."

Tully explained his dissertation.

Wilbur listened patiently. Unlike the people at the senior center he understood what a dissertation was.

When Tully was finished, Wilbur rose, went to the kitchen, returned with the coffee pot, and refilled their cups. Then he sat again at the table.

"I expect you already know most of what I'm going to tell you, but I might put a different slant on things. Before bean farming, this area was open range supporting a few cattle and sheep ranches. Up near the mountains the villagers had a little subsistence agriculture and woodcutting, as they had for a couple of hundred years.

"Everything changed in the early 1920s, when the Atchison, Topeka, and Santa Fe Rail Way put in a line through the valley and connected up with railroads in Belen. The open range disappeared, ranches were fenced, and the land was open to homesteading. It was a wet turn in the climate, and farmers began replacing ranchers. My father and mother moved out here from Kansas in 1934. I was born in this house, the oldest of eight children. I'm the only one still alive. Three died as infants.

"Pinto beans were what the farmers needed. They'd tried growing Irish potatoes, but disease wiped them out. Beans could survive in the dry climate with short growing seasons—if the climate wasn't too dry or the growing season too short. And beans stored well, and there was always a ready market for them, at good prices. In fact, if everything went right and there was a bumper crop, a farmer could get rich, almost overnight. It was like striking pay-dirt in a mine."

Wendy and Tully exchanged glances.

Wilbur continued. "But usually all that money just went to paying off debts from years when things didn't go right, which was most of the time.

"No, beans made this country around here—and they

broke it. A lot of homesteaders could have hung on longer if they'd planted other crops beside beans, but they were so dazzled by the potential riches that they only planted beans.

"When I was a kid here we had lots of neighbors. I could show you the foundations of the rural school we kids walked to. One by one our neighbors, bean farmers, all went bust and left. My family did things differently. We diversified, planted gardens, had domestic animals for meat and milk and eggs. We ran a few cattle and sheep. And we hung on. We still grew beans, but we weren't totally dependent on them. Dad and I both worked in town, when there was a town to work in. We worked at the bean husking plant, until it closed, then we bid on a rural postal route and ran that for a number of years. Sometimes I cowboyed at local ranches, helping during roundups, but we had to be really desperate to accept cowboy wages.

"Now I farm the government. I get Social Security and rural assistance checks a lot more regularly than we ever got bean checks. I'm the only one left out here. I never married, never met a woman who was willing to share this life. Can't say I blame them. But it's all I've ever known, and it suits me."

Tully spoke first. "Thank you so much for sharing your information, and your story, with us. I knew the basic outline of the bean economy here, but I didn't know the details, or how it affected actual people's lives."

Wilbur sipped his coffee. "That's the trouble with most history, it's all outline. But history isn't really like that. It's a structure built of individual decisions made by individual people. We're all part of history, whether we know it or not."

Wendy smiled sympathetically. "It was a hard life here. Today it's difficult for us to understand that kind of hardship. Yesterday we stopped by an abandoned homestead, off of County Road 46 on the way to Pleasant Valley. I took photographs. Do you happen to know anything about the people who lived there?"

"There's lots of abandoned homesteads along that road. Could you describe it a little better?"

Wendy did.

"Your description matches the Rollins place. Is the roof still on?"

Wendy nodded.

"Yep, that'd be the Rollins place. They hung on through the War—"

"We found old newspapers stuffed in the walls that mentioned the War," Tully interrupted.

"Yep, that cinches it, the Rollins place. They were among the last to go. They were nice folks, but they made the mistake of betting everything on beans."

Tully looked around the room in which they sat, at the primitive furniture, the bare-board walls, the absence of electronics. "It was a hard life, a hard life."

Wilbur watched Tully's survey. "Actually, this place here was on the upscale side of things."

Wendy put out her hand and touched his. "No, we weren't putting this place down. This place is way up from the Rollins place."

"Even that wasn't as rough as some," Wilbur continued. "If you want to see real hard living, I could take you out to the Laguna Salada area, the salt flats. That's always been the most miserable patch of land in these parts. There was only one farmer ever attempted to make a go of it out there, Oscar Bollinger.

"If you poke around here long enough you'll probably hear it, so I might as well tell you. He'd come into town at harvest time with the biggest beans you ever saw—and lots of them. It didn't matter how the weather went that year, he always had a bumper crop. Nobody'd ever seen beans like those, not around here.

"We all begged him to sell us some fertile ones so we could grow them too—all the beans he sold were infertile— but he never would, said those beans were his and his alone. I met him, cranky old buzzard, ugly as the back side of a cow, felt he'd been mistreated by the world, kept to himself.

"He hinted that he kept caches of fertile beans, and he left a few clues to tantalize folks. After he disappeared, presumably died somewhere, people went searching at his place and thereabouts, but they never found anything. People searched for years. Then beans faded in general, and it faded from most folks' memories. I'm probably one of the last who remembers."

Tully's eyes were wide. "But those beans couldn't still germinate, could they?"

"Depends on how they were stored. Beans'll keep a long time if they're kept cool and dry. In fact, there's a variety of bean, the 1500-Year Cave Bean, that's descended from three beans in a sealed clay pot found during an excavation of a cliff dwelling here in the Southwest."

Tully turned to Wendy, his eyes bright with excitement. "The Lost Pinto."

Wilbur continued, "When we were kids we spent a lot of time looking for his cache of beans—and it was all wasted time, except for the adventures and fun we had.

Sorry to burst your bubble, son, but later folks found out Oscar Bollinger financed those beans by robbing banks. He'd buy beans back in the Midwest, that was why they didn't sprout here, then bring them here to sell them. He was using those beans to launder bank money.

"Of course, no one knew what he did with the rest of the money. Maybe he hid it somewhere, buried it in a wooden box. But more likely he drank it up in bars in Albuquerque. He sure didn't spend it improving his place."

CHAPTER 7

"The Lost Pinto Treasure!" gasped Samster. "Wow!"

He sat cross-legged on the floor of Tully's apartment, next to an empty pizza box. Wendy reclined in the room's most comfortable chair, a curb-rescued La-Z-Boy. Tully sat at the table while Howdy dozed near the pizza box.

"Yep, the Lost Pinto Treasure," Tully said. "I'm not kidding. Somewhere out there in the dry lakes country is a fortune waiting to be discovered."

Samster looked at Wendy. "Is it true that there's a cache of stolen bank money out there?"

Now Tully was offended. Why did Samster ask Wendy? Didn't *he* have credibility?

Wendy glanced at Tully. "No, what Tully's saying is that there *might* be a cache of the money this hardscrabble farmer got from selling beans he bought with stolen bank money."

Then seeing hurt on Tully's face she added, "Tully's just telling you what the old farmer told us. He seemed pretty straightforward. He didn't actually say the money was out there, just that no one knew what the farmer did with his money. There's a difference. For all anyone knows, he blew it all on benders."

"Not all such tales are bullshit," Tully said to Wendy. "Besides, Wilbur Frost said he and his brother spent time looking for it in caves out there."

"Caves!" gasped Samster. "I love it! Secret caves, with

stashes of bank money"—"Bean money," Wendy interjected—
"with maybe an old chest and the bones of a farmer killed to
protect them and a curse placed on them and a treasure
map with a big bean drawn on it and Apaches still lurking
around to protect their secret." He laughed.

Tully laughed too. "Okay, okay I will admit it lends
itself to parody, and I'm not saying this exists, only
repeating what Wilbur Frost told us. You have to admit it's
a good story."

#

After Samster left, Tully turned to Wendy. "What do
you think?"

"About what?"

"The Lost Pinto Treasure?"

Wendy shook her head. "I think finishing your degree
and us getting married is a great idea." Tully looked
puzzled. Wendy continued. "I think the Lost Pinto
Treasure, or whatever you call it, is just another
distraction, like the lost mines. That's what I think."

Tully looked at her, then reached over and placed his
hand on hers. "You're right." This was not the time to argue
with her. "But it is an interesting element to the bean
story," he said, and chuckled. "One I hadn't expected to
find."

Wendy's shook her head. "What about the Rollins
family, who lived in that miserable homestead? Weren't
they interesting? And the boys having to go and herd cows
for meager wages? The mother raising a family there, with
no neighbors nearby and no modern conveniences? Weren't
they interesting?"

Before Tully could stammer a reply she shook her head and said, "So what's next? Will we all go on a Pinto Bean Treasure hunt with some Crazy Homer the Farmer, like Crazy Tony the Miner? Are you going to find a dried-up bean and put it in a locket and give it to me?" She crossed her arms over her chest and stared at him.

Tully just stared back. Her eyes were moist, her lips trembling. He'd never seen an outburst like this from Wendy before.

She uncrossed her arms. "I'm sorry, Tully, but I'm afraid that you'll never finish your dissertation, that we'll never get married, that our marriage plans will wind up being like these lost treasures of yours, wasting time and energy and always remaining just beyond reach."

She got up from the table and grabbed her shoulder bag. "I'm sorry, Tully, I really am. I know how much these things mean to you. I just wish our future together meant as much." She turned and left the apartment, slamming the door behind her.

Tully sat stunned. Then he leaped up and ran out the door. Wendy was getting into her car. "Wait! Wait."

Suddenly a fear he'd never experienced before gripped him. He couldn't let her just drive off. Barefoot and running through the sprinkler he dashed up to her. Dripping wet he pounded on her car's window.

"Wait, Wendy." She opened the window. "Listen, you're right, about everything. I don't want to lose you. Let's end all the doubt right now. Let's elope, just go off and get married, right now. Okay?"

Wendy was silent. Then finally, in a dull voice that shook Tully to his core, "You just don't get it. Don't you see that running off on the spur-of-the-moment to get married is just another impractical, romantic notion? What will we do, get married in an Elvis chapel in Las Vegas? Then move into your apartment? Alienate our families? I don't doubt your sincerity, but I don't want our marriage to be just another impulsive act of romantic fancy but the beginning of a serious, long-term commitment. We're not teenagers anymore."

Then she started the car and drove off.

Back in his apartment Tully lowered himself to the floor, collapsed against the La-Z-Boy. Blankly he looked around his disheveled apartment, caught a whiff of unwashed clothing, food left out too long, heard rap music being played on his neighbor's boom box. Run away and elope and return to *this*?

Wendy was right. How could he have been so blind not to have seen it? She'd been so patient and loving—and he'd been so insensitive and obtuse.

Why was he dragging his feet on his dissertation? And getting married? Was it as simple as not wanting to grow up? That was part of it, he knew. Even in high school, when his friends had moved on to girls and cars, he'd remained obsessed with looking for dinosaur bones and collecting stamps. That was one reason he'd always loved Wendy: she'd accepted him, made no demands on him to fit in with everyone else. And he'd taken her love for granted and abused her loyalty.

Now he was on the brink of losing everything. Of losing Wendy. More than once Elnora had hinted he could be dropped from the history department's doctoral program if he didn't get serious.

The time to grow up finally had come, but could he? What was life without the glamor of a mystery?

#

Samster pondered Tully's Pinto Bean Treasure story as he left on his bicycle. Slaloming effortlessly through the maze of campus sidewalks and pedestrians, he didn't evaluate the story's likelihood, only what a cache of cash would mean for him and his family.

Elron could go to college and study electrical engineering. Mom could quit her job and not have to take in loser boarders like Richard, maybe have a life again.

Maybe *he* could have a life.

He paused in his thinking to savor the focused rush of shushing down the steep, torturous street leading away from campus.

When he resumed thinking, he wondered what he would do with sudden wealth. And it disturbed him that he didn't immediately know. He'd always told himself he already had everything he needed or wanted, but that wasn't true. Some things were missing.

Maybe he could build a little cabin up in the mountains, with solar power, a windmill, water collection tanks, a composting outdoor toilet. He could live off the grid, just by himself, with his friends coming by to visit. Or maybe he could buy a nice guitar and learn to play it. Yes, he could use a little money for that. But was that all? He knew it wasn't.

#

A light tap at her office door caused Elnora Atkins to look up from her desk. "Hello, Tully." She tried not to show her puzzlement; Tully rarely stopped by her office.

"I don't mean to interrupt, and I won't take much of your time. I've got a quick question."

Now Elnora tried to conceal surprise. "Come in, Tully, sit down. I'm not doing anything that can't wait."

Tully hung the bicycle messenger bag he was carrying over the back of a chair facing Elnora, sat down, scratched his cheek, brushed a shock of hair from in front of his eyes, then looked up. "I'm considering photos and illustrations. I know the main focus of the dissertation will be the economic aspects of bean farming, but Wendy and I took a field trip to the area last weekend, and she took excellent photos of abandoned homesteads and the little towns and the natural environment. She's a talented photographer, takes it very seriously, and I'd like to use her work to show the human and environmental dimensions of bean farming. I think I know where I can get vintage photos of the area as well."

"Tully, that's a great idea. Photos could make a substantial contribution, give it depth that statistics would miss. You'd identify Wendy as the photographer, so she'd get credit. I'm curious, where exactly did you go last weekend?"

Tully relaxed into the chair, then began describing Pleasant Valley, bingo at the senior center, visiting the abandoned homesteads, interviewing Wilbur Frost.

Elnora looked at him carefully as he spoke. This Tully was very different from the sullen, reluctant student she'd seen recently. Why the change?

"And then he told us about this crazy old farmer and how he'd show up with huge mystery beans that later were discovered to have been bought with stolen bank money.

"The farmer's cache of bank loot is still out there."

Elnora frowned. "Tully, that's an interesting bit of folklore, and I'm happy your attitude toward your research has improved, but do remember: this is about economics, not folklore."

Tully leaned forward. "I understand, but you just said the human element would add depth to the economic discussion."

"And so it will. But only if you don't allow it to take over. I'm confident you have the ability to blend the human and the statistical into a narrative of great interest, but you also are easily distracted by the romantic and the fanciful—and hidden bank loot has the makings of a distraction."

"You and Wendy should get together," Tully muttered under his breath.

"What?"

"Nothing. Look, I understand what you're saying, and I promise to keep focused."

"I have a suggestion. Why don't you go to the State Records Center and Archives in Santa Fe? I'll give you a letter of introduction. If you've never worked in the archives before, you'll enjoy it. It's to historians what a gold vein is to prospectors." She paused, then smiled. "Maybe that isn't the best analogy."

Tully raised an eyebrow.

"The photo archive is part of the Southwest History collection. Most of the books are limited editions or out-of-print or one-of-a-kind documents. When you get to the collection," she continued, "ask for Roland. Tell him I referred you. He's been with the collection longer than most of the books. He can help you find things you wouldn't find on your own."

"Roland. Okay."

"Good hunting, Tully—and let me know what you find."

#

After Tully left, Elnora scribbled notes on a pad: the town Tully had visited, the homesteaders' cabins, Wilbur Frost. Then she stared at the pad. What had Tully meant when he said "You and Wendy should get together." Had something occurred on the trip between him and Wendy? She hoped not. Wendy was good for him, even if Elnora suspected her of being too passive.

CHAPTER 8

Wendy scowled as she approached the table in the student union building where Tully and Samster sat looking at a scatter of papers. Since their argument she'd remained cool toward him. She knew Tully was trying to make amends, but just as she was slow to anger, she also was slow to reconcile.

Tully looked up as she approached and smiled brightly, perhaps too brightly. "Look at what Samster has."

"Looks like a mess of papers." She smiled warmly at Samster, who returned her warmth.

"I think I've mentioned my great-aunt, Conchita, who lives in Jarales south of Belen. She just turned ninety, and the family felt if would be best if she went to live with her sister, Elena, who's only eighty-five. She lives in an old adobe in Casa Colorada.

"So last weekend I went to join a bunch of my relatives in moving Conchita. She was a hoarder. If something came her way, she kept it. I half expected to find Coronado's saddle in one of her closets." Wendy nodded; Samster and Tully were packrats too.

"So anyway, in one closet was a box of old maps, documents, and stuff, so I thought I'd take them to show Tully, being the historian that he is."

Wendy knew Tully and Samster shared a passion for old documents and recalled his excitement when he found the old newspapers and magazines at the Rollins homestead.

Riffling through the brittle, yellowed documents on the table Tully said, "These are from the 1880s. Let's see, payment of taxes receipt, delinquent payment of taxes, a lien on property, a filing of sale of property, notice of intent to extend a street, list of property owners—I'm sorry, Samster, I don't think any of this gives us title to the state capitol."

"Bummer. I was counting on being able to move Richard Lone Elk to the Round House."

From the large manila envelope beside him Samster took more papers. "Are these mining claims?" He pointed to thin sheets on which were drawn a kaleidoscope of polygons, with hand-lettered measurements and labels.

Tully glanced at a couple of them. "Looks like it. But don't get excited. Those old prospectors filed a claim on any property with more than five rocks on it. That way they were covered if something valuable actually was found. Invariably, nothing was, so they just let the claims lapse.

"It was fairly cheap and easy to file a claim, and all you had to do was perform a token amount of work on it each year. You didn't have to actually produce ore, just dig a hole to prove the claim was active. Then next year dig another hole. You could keep a claim indefinitely if you did that, but after a while it wasn't worth the bother, especially if you had numerous claims and they also were bust. If you actually found a valuable ore body, you'd patent your claim. It was more complicated and expensive, but then you owned the land."

"So these claim maps are just maps to dry holes?"

"I'm afraid so. The Bureau of Geology or the local historical society might want them, for their historical value, but even that wouldn't be much, given how many of these charts were floating around. Every miner and prospector had several sets."

Samster said, "Hey, Tully, you could use these to paper the walls of your apartment. Instead of dry wall you'd have dry hole."

Wendy frowned. This conversation didn't interest her at all, in fact it veered into territory she'd prefer Tully avoid.

Tully didn't look up. "Very funny." He continued thumbing through the claim maps. "I'm looking for landmarks. Sometimes these maps show roads and sites that have vanished from modern maps. That can be pretty interesting."

Samster also inspected the maps. He turned one over. "Hey, there's another map on the back of this one. It looks hand drawn."

Tully and Wendy leaned over. Tully traced the marks with his finger. "This isn't a claim map."

Wendy looked closer. "You're right. There are no claim boundaries or measurements. It's just a map."

"But to what?" said Samster.

"It shows a range of mountains, or part of a range, and what looks like a trail leading into them," said Tully.

Samster now was interested. "Read what the lettering says."

Tully leaned closer. "It's pretty faint, and it was done with a pencil. I can't make out all the words. I think this says 'spring.' Here's another one labeled 'spring.' These jagged lines look they're meant to indicate a ridge, and this word looks like 'dacite.'"

"What's that?" asked Samster.

"A kind of rock, volcanic. Pretty common in most of New Mexico."

"You don't think he meant to write 'diamonds?'"

Tully chuckled. "Nice try. 'Dirt' maybe. And these lines indicate drainages. I think this one says 'shaped like a ...'" I can't read the rest."

"What about this word here?" asked Samster.

Tully looked closely. "I think it says 'QTQ.'"

Samster shook his head. "That doesn't make any sense."

Samster's brow furrowed. "Let's see, it could be the initials of the person who made the map. You know, Quincy Tecumseh Quatermain."

"I think it's a surveyor's mark. The claim map on the other side was drawn by a surveyor, and it makes sense he'd scribble a map and a survey symbol on the back."

"Makes sense," said Samster. Wendy looked bored. For all she cared they could be discussing clues in a video game.

"It would be fun to try to find the place the hand-drawn map was pointing to. If we could just identify which reference grid the surveyor was using, it should be fairly easy to get coordinates and find it using a GPS unit."

Wendy scowled. "Sounds like a waste of time to me."

"Aw, come on, Wendy," said Tully, "didn't you ever go on a scavenger hunt as kid?"

She remained stubbornly silent.

"I think it'd be fun," said Samster. "We could ask Crazy Tony about the map, I'll bet he'd know what the letters mean."

"At least he might know the location that surveyor's marker refers to," said Tully.

Now Wendy glared at Tully. Then in a voice she normally used for pre-school children struggling with the concept of flushing the toilet she said, "Give it up, Tully, you should have more important things on your mind."

Samster said, "I'll show it to Elron, he's good at figuring out things like that."

#

That night Tully received a call from Samster. "I showed that map to Elron. We spent an hour trying to figure out what those letters, QTQ, referred to. After some time on the internet we're pretty sure they have nothing do with surveying."

"We they've got to mean something."

"They do. Elron figured it out, based on his experience as a gamer. It's a code."

"A code?"

"Move each letter backward two positions in the alphabet."

"*Q* becomes *O* So it spells *oro*."

"Which is the Spanish word for—"

"Gold."

CHAPTER 9

Tully felt a satisfying nudge from his seat as the commuter train to Santa Fe lurched away from the station in downtown Albuquerque. He smiled and relaxed. As many times as he had made the trip he still enjoyed it. He was a historian, after all, and the train traveled roughly the same route to Santa Fe traveled by the earliest Spanish conquistadors and explorers more than 450 years ago.

The Spaniards had arrived at an abandoned Indian pueblo, on a perennial stream at the base of the Sangre de Cristo Mountains; they didn't stay but continued north to an inhabited pueblo. Twelve years later they were back at what became Santa Fe.

The train slid smoothly north, Tully observing the sites of the Indian pueblos the Spaniards had encountered. Some were still inhabited: Sandia, Santa Ana, San Felipe, Kewa, Cochiti. Many more had been inhabited when the Spaniards arrived—Alameda, Puaray, Kuaua, Tonque, La Bajada—but with the arrival of the pale, bearded strangers their days were numbered.

For in each pueblo, in each Indian village, the Spaniards had asked the same question: *Oro? Donde está el oro?* "Gold? Where is the gold?"

Oro. Gold. That's what the map had said. After agreeing that it was a code, albeit a primitive one, Samster had exclaimed, "It's a treasure map!"

Tully's response was slightly more restrained—"It *appears* to be a map to a gold deposit, that's for sure."—but his mind was frothing just like Samster's.

"We have to use the map to find it," Samster had said.

"We do," Tully had agreed, "but ..." In his mind the map's image had superimposed on it the image of Wendy stalking away angry and disgusted. Then the image of Elnora appeared. "This couldn't come at a worse time," he said.

"What? Stumbling upon a map to a gold mine is bad timing? Maybe for you, dude, but not for me."

They'd hung up agreeing that somehow they had to find time to investigate the map, but they also had to be creative in how they did it so as not to jeopardize other priorities. Tully felt a twinge of guilt over that, but he realized that categorizing Wendy as just a "priority" made him even more uncomfortable.

#

Tully stared out the window and watched as the train glided by San Felipe Pueblo across the Rio Grande. With its modest adobe buildings it probably appeared not much different now from how Coronado would have seen it in 1540, when he arrived, asking where's the gold?

He thought of the Spaniards. They too had been on a treasure hunt. And why not? Hadn't Esteban the Moor, the first European to enter the unknown land to the north, returned to Mexico saying he'd seen cities of gold? Nor was the Spaniards' belief in golden cities shaken when they later discovered that the Indian villages actually were built of mud and stone, not gold, for hadn't Cortez discovered an Indian empire rich with gold beyond imagining? Was this not a *Nuevo Mejico?* Gold *had* to be here, just a little farther, always a little farther.

As the train left the pueblos behind to wind around the escarpment known as La Bajada, Tully's mind again alighted on the hand-drawn map with the letters QTQ written on it. His life would be much simpler if in fact it had been just a surveyor's marker.

But the map's sketch of the mountains? All the documents in Conchita's box had come from the Socorro area—but which range? Several were in the region. The mountains on the map weren't just a generic zigzag symbol but rather had a deliberately drawn outline, with some features and profiles that should be recognizable—but from where?

Maybe Crazy Tony would know, but instinct told Tully it would be best not to mention the map to Crazy Tony.

Wendy. He needed to repair his relationship with her. She was right: she'd been patient long enough. He'd change. He'd be more sensitive, more attentive. He really would. In fact, he'd be sure to bring her a present from Santa Fe.

#

The rail line terminated near the old train station in Santa Fe, just a few yards from the State Records Center and Archives. The center was open. Behind a security desk an elderly Hispanic man sat reading a newspaper. He looked at Tully.

"Good morning," said Tully, with a brightness he didn't feel. "I'm here to use the archive." From his book bag he extracted Elnora's letter introducing him.

The security guard didn't glance at it but rather simply turned the register around so Tully could sign in. Tully looked at the corridors leading from the entrance.

"Which way to the Archives?"

The security guard nodded to his left. Above the doorway was an arrow and a sign labeled "Archives."

As Tully left, the guard returned to his newspaper. Tully told himself the guard routinely saw dozens of people miss the sign—no big deal. He still felt stupid.

The door opened onto a long corridor flanked by offices: State Records, Land Grant Documents, Genealogy, Curator of Deeds and Property, Translation and Documentation, Micrographics ... Tully shook his head. Should he be looking for an office reading "Curator of Beans"?

The corridor ended at a set of double doors with frosted glass panes on which was printed in antique Gothic gold lettering "Archives—Archivos." Tully pushed open the door and faced another security desk. Behind this one sat a middle-aged Hispanic woman.

"May I help you?" she said.

Putting on his most winning smile, Tully said, "I'm here for the local history collection."

The woman smiled. "You know what they say, 'All history is local.' Do you have a specific region or subject you're interested in?"

"Well, for starters, I'm interested in New Mexico minerals."

The smile sagged into a knowing frown. "I see. You're a treasure-hunter."

"What do you mean?"

"We get at least one of you a week. You come in here asking for documents relating to someplace associated with minerals and mining, but you're really trying to track down some lost treasure. There's one over there."

She nodded toward a table at which man of indeterminate late middle age stood looking over a table on which maps were spread. He wore a flannel shirt and Carhartt overalls while on his head was a ball cap labeled Conway Scrap Metals. In his hands held vertically were two six-inch lengths of pipe from which protruded two rods, bent into a right angle. He was moving them over the maps.

"What's he doing?"

The receptionist just shrugged, so Tully walked over and in his most polite voice asked, "Excuse me sir, may I ask what you're doing?"

The man stopped moving the rods and looked at Tully with a mixture of suspicion and contempt. Finally he said, "I'm prospecting, so don't get too close."

"Prospecting?"

"Map dowsing," the man growled. Seeing Tully's bewilderment, he continued, "You've heard of water dowsing I take it?"

Tully nodded.

"Well, you can dowse for anything, if you've got the gift—and I do."

"You're looking for a map?"

"Hell no, you young fool. I'm looking for what's in the area shown on the map. Precious metals."

Still seeing bewilderment, the man continued, "If you hold these rods over barren ground, the rods just swing randomly, but move 'em over an ore deposit, the rods cross, like the crosshairs in a rifle sight. You mark that, and that's where you go."

"Wow! Who'd have thought it? Are you finding anything?"

"You think I'd tell you? Now keep your distance, I don't want you looking over my shoulder."

Tully walked back to the receptionist. "You wouldn't believe what that guy was doing."

"Yes I would. As long as they don't bring in eye of newt or bat's blood and damage the resources, they can do whatever they want. But we have to watch you, you treasure hunters rummage around for a while, make a mess of things, expecting to find some hand-drawn map or some prospector's diary that's going to point to the Great Bonanza. Then a week later someone else comes in and asks the same thing. You're a treasure hunter."

Tully reddened. The woman's accusation was partly true. If in seeking information he also could find something relating to gold-mining in the mountains near Socorro, so much the better. He hadn't forgotten the old map.

The woman continued. "Well, we can't refuse anyone, so you can look, but because of theft and vandalism, people stealing documents and tearing pages out of publications, we have some restrictions. You're not allowed in the stacks, and all materials have to be examined over there." She nodded to another table.

Tully tried to repair his image. "Actually, I'm not a treasure hunter. I've always been interested in geology, and I thought that as long as I was here ..."

The woman gave him no quarter but just stared at him as if to say, "Sure, sure."

"I'm not a treasure hunter, honest, I'm a doctoral candidate in Western History at the University of New Mexico. Here." He rummaged in his bag for Elnora's letter, which he held out to her.

She looked at it, then at him, her eyebrows raised, some of her disgust dissipating.

"Okay, I admit am interested in treasure"—her frown returned—"but as an historian, not as someone who's out to find it." Seeing a redeeming opening he plunged ahead. "Actually, I'd like to interview you sometime, regarding the treasure-hunters you've met here. I imagine they're quite a bunch."

"They are that."

"My main purpose in being here is bean-farming research, the subject of my dissertation."

Confusion now replaced skepticism on the woman's face.

"Elnora said I should ask for someone named Roland."

Tully sensed her softening. She glanced at Elnora's letter. "Your name is Tully?"

Tully gave an appealing, sheepish grin. "It's short for Tulburt, my last name, but my first name is Wilford, and I think you'll agree Tully is better than either of those. And your name is Maria?" He'd glanced at the brass name plate on her desk: Maria Trujillo. "Maybe it's short for Mariachankowsky?"

This succeeded in eliciting a chuckle as she rose from her chair. "Wait here, Tully, I'll go get Roland."

#

Roland was not what Tully expected. Instead of a small, gnomish man like others he had known from the university library, the man was a giant sloth who dwarfed the receptionist. He wore shapeless brown pants that could not recall their last crease and a bulky green sweater. His hair, what remained of it, was gray and needed trimming. The length of his lugubrious face was accentuated by the longest earlobes Tully had ever seen. He shambled across the room in shoes at least twice the size of Tully's.

"This is Tully, a student of Elnora Atkins's." She handed Roland the introductory letter.

Roland didn't glance at it but instead looked at Tully with deep-set eyes, and extended a hand that enveloped Tully's like a squid devouring a fish, though the grip was surprisingly gentle.

"Pleased to meet you," Roland said in a deep, slow voice. Now he looked at the letter.

"So you're doing dissertation research on Estancia Valley bean farming." It wasn't a question. Tully smiled and nodded.

Ignoring the smile, Roland continued. "That's an interesting area of research, one that's been neglected for too long. We don't have as many materials as we should have, but we do have some. Follow me, please." And with that he turned and returned to the open door from whence he had come.

#

The local history archive was a dimly lit warren of shelves, tables, and cabinets. Tully saw instantly why Elnora had urged him to seek out Roland.

With his head, the big man indicated Tully should sit at a table while he collected materials. Soon he returned with a stack of books and papers.

"This isn't all, but it's a good start. Let me know if you have any questions." And with that Roland disappeared back into the warren.

Tully took from his book bag his notebook computer, his leather ring-binder notebook, and several pens and pencils. Then he attacked the materials in front of him.

He decided to go for the newspaper clippings first. Tully always marveled that every community in New Mexico, even the smallest, had had at least one newspaper. It was as if information was as important as food and shelter in the early settlements. That was especially true, he knew, of mining camps, but it appeared farming communities were no different.

Moriarty and Estancia, the main surviving pinto bean centers, had hosted numerous newspapers over the years. Even Willard, now little more than a husk of a town, had two, the *Willard Record* and the *Willard Weekly News*. Tully started with these, because they'd been published during the early years of bean farming.

The stories mostly were accounts of bean harvests, fluctuations in the bean market, weather good and bad, the arrival of tractors and other implements, and construction of new storage facilities. But these stories appeared beside the community stories: birth notices, obituaries, marriages, the farmer injured while building a new barn, children's 4-H projects, church socials and barbecues, Grange activities, and the dedication of a new school.

The community was a human body; beans and the money they generated were the blood. Tully thought of the Rollins family, whose abandoned home he and Wendy had visited.

He looked at the photos. In the early days, people always stood stolidly facing the camera, with sober expressions and hands at their sides, postures that smudged individuality. But occasionally personality peered through the faded black-and-white photos.

He lingered at the photo of young man named Eduardo Duran, standing beside his bride in front of a small church. Did photographers then have a rule against smiling, even at weddings? Eduardo was a good ten years younger than Tully. People matured early then, he observed, then chose not to pursue the thought further.

Did he and Eduardo have *anything* in common? Possibly not language, for Eduardo certainly grew up in a Spanish-speaking home. Nor religion; Eduardo's conventional Catholicism was far from his fuzzy Buddhism. Nor education. Nor money. Nor work experience, nor interests, nor view of life, nor expectations of life, nor ...

Could he possibly be related to Samster Duran? And if so, the two could not be more different.

Tully wondered what happened to Eduardo.

#

During the morning and into the afternoon Tully alternated between newspapers and books and pamphlets. The real estate promotions were shameless. County directories gave an idea of where people lived and what goods and services they bought. And occasionally a booklet or monograph or diary would describe life in the area.

He had just finished one of these when Roland returned. "I hope you're finding what you need?"

I am. This stuff is fascinating. I especially like the self-published material."

"That's a wise preference. It's among those less-than-polished works that the true voices of history speak. The statistics, the directories, the reports—all those are like pottery sherds, they tell you nothing of the people whose lives they purport to record.

"You chose a good topic for your research. So much of Western History has been stampeded over by the drama mongers."

He paused and looked at Tully with his deep eyes. Tully could only nod.

"The cowboys and Indians—there was a lot of colorful history there, and real too, but that landscape has been so worked over you can't find the truth anymore. You're lucky, you're dealing with the virgin stuff of history. What the people here tell you"—he gave a slow, deliberate nod to the stack of materials—"is likely to be true."

He got up slowly to return into the archives. "There were a couple of diaries and family histories in the Hatcher collection. I'll get those for you."

When he left Tully realized that no computer database ever could be as quick or thorough as Roland's mind. And he also suspected Roland's life in the archive wasn't as lonely it might seem.

It was forty-five minutes to closing, and Tully was browsing the last of the family histories Roland had retrieved. As he picked one up he froze: *Torrance County Memories*, by Tom Frost.

Tully recalled what the bean-farmer Wilbur Frost had said: "At one time there were a lot of us here, but one way or another all of us moved on. Tom went on high. He's buried in the Willard Cemetery."

The booklet was a small, self-published collection of reminiscences of growing up and living as a bean farmer in the Estancia Valley. Several tales mentioned his brothers and sister, including Wilbur.

Tully read eagerly. Old Tom, in his folksy way and simple, direct style, gave life to the people of bean country. Tully read each chapter. He wondered if Tom Frost had known Eduardo Duran. For that matter, had Wilbur Frost ever known him?

Suddenly Tully had the afternoon's second heart-stopping moment: the chapter titled "A Torrance County Mystery" was about the Missing Farmer, Sam Bollinger.

"While I was still a lad on the farm, a mystery swept through the county that thrilled my young imagination. Sam Bollinger had disappeared. Nothing like this had happened before. All us boys knew who Sam Bollinger was: the crazy old farmer who lived by himself out by the salt pans and who it turned out robbed banks to finance bean-farming."

Glancing at the clock, Tully began scribbling frantically in his notebook. Tom told the story of the so-called mystery beans and Bollinger's mysterious disappearance.

He told that once when a farmer stopped by Bollinger's place, he found Bollinger's buggy but not Bollinger. The place looked recently lived in, and Bollinger's dogs, while ravenous and thirsty, were still alive.

A formal search was organized, but they found nothing. The police made inquiries. They too learned nothing. One moment Bollinger had been at his place, and the next he wasn't.

His unexplained disappearance galvanized everyone. Wherever people went, they looked for Bollinger or his body. In ditches, in groves of Siberian elms, in abandoned buildings, in cisterns—wherever the people looked they half-expected to confront the missing farmer's grisly remains. To a young boy, the horror was delicious.

"Tully, I'm afraid you'll have to come back. We're soon to close."

"Can I have one … no, two, more minutes?"

"I think I can spare that." Tully flipped to the chapter's ending:

"No one ever found anything. Sam Bollinger remained missing. Eventually people forgot about it, but long after people stopped searching for Bollinger's body they continued searching for his supposed cache of bank money, and I'll always remember the happy days I spent with Wilbur roaming around the salt lakes, never knowing what we'd find, but always having a keen adventure."

\#

All the way back to Albuquerque on the train Tully thought of nothing but the mystery of the farmer's disappearance and hidden stash of money. As he stepped from the train onto the platform he thought, "Wendy and I will have to pay Wilbur Frost another visit."

Then he remembered he had forgotten to get a gift for Wendy.

CHAPTER 10

The trip to the archives appeared to have motivated Tully, so two days after his trip to Santa Fe he and Wendy had agreed to another trip to Bean Country. Now, as she drove, with Tully beside her, Wendy struggled with conflicting emotions. Another field trip to Bean Country was a step in the right direction. She'd brought her camera gear, Tully his taping and recording equipment. Could be fun, the last trip was. At the least, it would keep him from haring off on that Socorro map thing. But she strongly suspected that what really excited him was the Lost Pinto Treasure, not the Lost Dissertation.

They slowed as they entered Pleasant Valley. "Should we stop?" she asked.

Tully answered her question with a blank stare.

"I mean, stop and pay a courtesy call to some of the people we met at the Senior Center."

They looked on both sides of Main Street as their car crept down the empty pavement, alert for any signs of life: lights in houses, the glow of a TV, chimneys smoking, pickups in driveways, livestock in pens. Nothing. Even dogs were absent.

"Let's skip the social call."

Wendy nodded. "Kind of creepy isn't it. A dead town that hasn't been pronounced dead."

"It's a zombie town."

They decided that enough daylight remained to visit Wilbur Frost. Two days ago Tully had called Henry Holland to relay a message to Wilbur that they would be coming on Saturday, and even arriving late was better than not showing at all.

She remembered all the twists and turns in the dirt road, so they arrived sooner than they'd expected. The dogs barked, and Wilbur emerged from the house, just as before.

"Come in and sit a spell. There's coffee inside."

As before the aroma of freshly brewed coffee greeted them as they followed the old homesteader into the now-familiar room. As Wilbur took the coffee pot from the top of the cast-iron stove, Tully said, "Mmmm! I just know coffee brewed over a wood fire tastes better than coffee from a fancy coffee maker." Wilbur smiled as he filled the cups on the table.

Tully explained that he had been to the archives. "I found your brother's book at the end of the day; they kicked me out before I could finish it. But I'll be back working in the archive, and I'll make it a priority."

"Tom always was the more educated member of the family, not that we didn't all go to school, it's just that he took to it more than the rest of us. I don't know what happened to all the copies of that book he had printed. Guess he gave 'em away or they wound up in collections somewhere, the kind of books that drift into antique and junk shops. I've got one around here somewhere, but it'd take me a week to find it. I'm happy one of 'em made its way to the archives."

Wendy sipped her coffee. "I haven't read the book, but from what Tully told me it sounds fascinating."

"Your brother had a natural gift for telling a story," Tully said. "The details he provided, the insights into life in that era, well, they're just invaluable, and I'm sure many of them will wind up in my dissertation. And, of course, his book will appear in the citations."

"He'd have appreciated that."

Wendy listened as Tully, activating his recorder and also scribbling notes in his notebook, interviewed Wilbur about homesteader days in bean country. She found Wilbur's reminiscences fascinating, the details of life before electricity, before telephones, before television and certainly before computers and the entire electronic world.

It was a world that most humans throughout history would have understood—raising crops, heating with wood, having gardens, depending on domestic animals for food and clothing, making music with instruments and voices, interacting face-to-face with other humans. It was all so traditional and natural, yet in less than a century it had passed from being normal life into the realm of anthropology, to be studied like a tribe of hunter-gatherers.

During a pause in Wilbur's narrative Tully asked, "Did you ever know someone named Eduardo Duran? In the archive I saw a newspaper photo of him taken at his wedding."

Wilbur put down his coffee cup and stared at it a long time. Wendy started to say something to ease the awkwardness when Wilbur said, "I'm afraid he was before my time."

Tully arched his eyebrows questioningly.

"I didn't know Eduardo, but his wife and three of their kids all died in the 1918 flu epidemic. It hit New Mexico pretty hard, 'specially rural areas like around here. There were no health facilities, no clinics, folks were pretty much on their own. Hell, until the flu hit, New Mexico was the only state in the union without a state department of health."

He paused, shook his head. "The first case of the flu was reported on October 7, 1917, the first fatality four days later. By a month later, there were 50,000 cases, and 5,000 people dead. And the state had only 360,000 people at the time. It spread across the state like a prairie fire in a high wind."

"That's terrible," said Wendy. "I had no idea, I mean, I'd heard about the 1918 flu, but ..."

"You wonder how I know so much about it, since I wasn't even born then? Obviously, my parents survived."

Tully and Wendy waited.

"Yes, they survived, but not all the Frosts did. I grew up without grandparents on my father's side, and only an old, bitter grandmother on my mom's side. The flu punched a lot of holes in my extended family.

"And everyone I knew had the same experience. It was as if the flu came through and swept away all the relatives and loved ones people had accumulated over generations. It was like a fire destroying the ancestral family home.

"Marie Duran was the only one of Eduardo's kids that survived. The rest of her family went into the Cedar Wells Cemetery. She was luckier than many survivors, she had some family in the area who took her in. She was about thirty when I knew her. She married an Espinosa boy, and they settled down near Corona. She and her husband would pass by our place from time to time selling piñon nuts and herbal remedies. She became a *curandera*, using traditional Hispanic herbal remedies to try to cure people who didn't have access to any other recourse. It was her calling. I don't know what happened to her."

Tully and Wendy sat in silence.

Wilbur continued staring at his coffee. Finally he looked up and said, "The flu affected bean-farming indirectly, because some farmers who were down on their luck just gave up and moved on. They never knew when another epidemic would come through and wipe them out. They wanted to live where there were better medical facilities. Can't say I blamed 'em."

Wendy and Tully both shook their heads sadly. Then Tully said, "Before we leave I want to ask about that farmer and his bean and bank money. Your brother wrote about him in his book."

Wilbur's face darkened. He paused before answering. "Forget Bollinger and his beans."

Tully's eyes showed surprise. "But your brother wrote about him in his book. It's a fascinating story, um ... from a folklore viewpoint. And that mystery was never solved. The money is still out there."

Wendy's frown now joined Wilbur's.

Wilbur shook his head with something more than disgust. "Forget Bollinger. A lot of people wasted a lot of time looking for the money, including me and my brother. And nobody ever had anything to show for it. He sure never spent any of it improving his place."

"But Tom said you and he had some good times together looking for it. It could be a fun, harmless little adventure."

"Funny thing about legends like that. They start out being fun and harmless, and then somewhere along the line they stop being fun—and they stop being harmless. Let 'em go."

"What do you ..."

But before he could finish Wendy abruptly stood. Looking directly at Tully she said, "We've taken enough of Mr. Frost's time, and it's getting late. We need to head back to Albuquerque." Then turning to Wilbur she said, "Thank you so much for your hospitality and your good information—and your coffee too. Tully, can I help you carry some of the books Mr. Frost loaned you out to the car?"

"Uh, that's okay, I can manage." He stood and gathered his gear. Extending his hand to Wilbur he said, "Wendy's right, I can't overstate what a help you've been. I ... didn't mean to be rude pressing about Bollinger, but ... well, you have to admit it's a good story."

Wilbur shook his hand, but said nothing, a look on his face that bespoke an inner pain.

As Tully and Wendy descended the steps, Wilbur softened. "The real treasure in these parts is still here. It's beans, just plain old ordinary pinto beans. Come back any time if I can be of more help."

#

As soon as their car was out of sight of Wilbur's homestead, Tully turned to Wendy. "What the hell was all that?"

"I don't know what triggered Wilbur's reaction, but pushing him down a path he didn't want to go was just plain rude. I know you didn't mean anything, but this whole treasure obsession of yours is getting out of hand. It's messing with your dissertation—and it's messing with us. Wilbur gave you some good advice. I hope you listened."

CHAPTER 11

"They look lonely." Samster nodded toward the mountains far to the east of Interstate-25. He and Tully sat in Samster's mother's twenty-year-old Toyota Tercel driving south toward Socorro.

Tully looked across the Rio Grande valley at the distant ranges. A haze hung over the broad basin, making the mountains appear as through frosted glass, ethereal and remote.

"They *are* lonely," Tully answered. "No one lives in them, not even a few stubborn ranchers. Wealthy sheep owners living in the towns along the river used to send shepherds and flocks out there. They'd build primitive sheep camps if they found springs, but even the shepherds didn't get into the mountains, unless sheep strayed there. Too barren. There are a few plants even sheep won't eat. And until the late nineteenth century Apaches made the mountains too dangerous, not that the Indians were overly fond of the mountains either, except as hideouts."

Tully looked at his friend gazing eastward. He knew what Samster was thinking. Distant desert ranges, floating like mirages, had the same effect on him. They were mountains of myth and mystery, keepers of secrets. He recalled one evening driving east toward the Guadalupe Mountains in southeastern New Mexico as the setting sun burnished the limestone cliffs to a rich gold.

In the 1870s the old prospector, Ben Sublette, claimed to have found a rich source of gold in the Guadalupes that no one has found since. The Lost Sublette Treasure. That the mountains were made of limestone didn't bother most treasure seekers, but Tully knew from geology those ancient reef-building corals were secreting calcium, not precious metals. Nonetheless, when he saw those cliffs, golden and forbidding, he felt the mountains themselves had the power to secrete gold, even if the corals didn't. There had to be hidden treasure there, there just *had* to be.

As if to confirm Tully's thoughts Samster said, "You don't suppose those might be the mountains shown on the map?"

"Could be, could be. It does seem the more remote, rugged, and inaccessible a range is, the more hidden gold it has."

"What are the mountains' names?"

"Hard to identify them from this distance, but, let's see, there's the Oscura Mountains, or "the Dark Mountains," the Sierra del Sombre, "Mountains of the Shadow," the San Andres Mountains, and those far in the distance might be the Sacramento Mountains. There are some minor ranges as well."

"Well, if the mountains are 'remote, rugged, and inaccessible,' as you say, that's why their gold hasn't been discovered yet."

"There was no place too rugged or remote for those old prospectors." Wanting to change the subject Tully said, "I feel pretty bad not inviting Wendy along. Not that she'd have wanted to come."

"Yeah, she's pretty down on the whole treasure thing. I guess I can understand how she feels."

"What's that supposed to mean?"

"Chill, dude, I just know that she loves you, and wants things to work out for you—and her."

"Well, so do I. Driving down here to Socorro to check out some old county records isn't exactly going to torpedo our relationship, or my career. And you're here too."

"Yeah, but I don't have a girlfriend, or a career."

That comment landed between them with a heavy thud, and both fell silent.

#

In Socorro they drove to the building on the town's plaza that housed the county offices. Inside they followed directions to the records office where the bored young woman behind the counter gave them the news Tully had half-expected: "We don't have anything from that long ago, everything was lost after the original courthouse was torn down in the 1950s."

But after they'd thanked her and were slouching out the door she called, "You might try the Bureau of Geology over at Tech. I think a lot of that old stuff wound up over there."

#

The New Mexico Bureau of Geology, located on the campus of the New Mexico Institute of Mining and Technology, was a three-story angular building. Inside the receptionist directed them to the basement.

When they passed through the double wooden doors, they entered a square room the size of a basketball court, appearing smaller by being crammed with desks, bookshelves, and map cases. The room's silence hung like dust, and like the archive in Santa Fe it had the dry smell peculiar to old paper. Behind the desk near the entrance a diminutive white-haired woman sat, the only person in the room. She looked up when they approached.

"We're interested in records pertaining to nineteenth-century mining claims," Tully said in his most pleasant voice, whereupon the librarian did something Tully hadn't thought possible: she rolled her eyes without actually moving her eyes.

Annoyed, Tully said, "I'm a doctoral candidate in the history department at UNM." He wanted to say he wasn't a treasure hunter, but he couldn't quite do that, not with Samster there. Instead he said, "I'm going through archives in the state. I was at the archives in Santa Fe last week. Roland was a great help, maybe you know him?"

Instantly the woman brightened. "Roland, indeed I do, he was invaluable to me when I took over the position here. You wouldn't believe the mess things were in, but with his wise counsel we've got things pretty much in order. I hope I can be as much help. My name is Esther."

Tully introduced himself and Samster.

"Are you a historian too?" she asked Samster.

"Only in the sense that I try to find out what went wrong with bicycles. I work at a bike shop near UNM."

"Samster, that's an odd nickname, does it come from Samuel? You'd be surprised how many parents choose that name from the Bible for their sons."

Samster showed a sheepish smile. "It's from the Bible all right, Samson, as in Delilah, but my friends called me Samster, and I decided I liked that better than Samson."

"Can't say I blame you," said Esther.

Tully knew this, of course, and also that while his friend didn't reveal this to most people, he was proud of his odd nickname, felt it gave him distinction.

"Well, since we're now all on a first-name basis, what can I help you with?"

They unrolled the thin, yellowed sheet. "We're trying to identify the miner who filed these claims. We're not looking for the mines themselves, and even if we were I know enough mining history to know that all we'd likely find would be just an abandoned prospect hole."

Esther frowned. "This could be difficult."

"I know there were hundreds of these sheets floating around."

"It's worse than that. At the time this was made, Socorro County was much larger than it is now. It went all the way to the Arizona border. It was larger than some states, with dozens of mining districts, but maybe we can narrow it down a bit."

While Tully and Samster wandered around the room, looking at framed maps and documents on the wall, Esther scrutinized the map and made some notes. Then she went to a tall flat-file case, where she pulled out a drawer and riffled through several maps until she found the one she wanted. She scribbled more notes, then motioned for Tully and Samster.

"You're in luck. A few years back Dick Everly, the Bureau's mining historian then, began an inventory of claims for which there were records, starting with the area right around Socorro, so he could field-check if he needed to. This was back in the fifties, not long after the courthouse was demolished. He didn't get very far before a new director gave him another project, but your claims were within his area."

Tully and Samster drew closer. "What information did he collect?" asked Tully.

"Dick Everly was nothing if not thorough. Let's see here. He noted the claim's location, the date it was filed, by whom, the mineral the claim was for, and what work had been done on it."

"And? ..." asked Samster eagerly.

"Your claim was in the Chupadera Mountains, there was a lot of mining activity in that area at one time, mostly for lead and silver, though your prospector just listed 'precious metals.' A lot of them did that, especially if they didn't know what might actually be there. It doesn't appear any work was done on it. It was filed November 17, 1875, the prospector was Lester Toler."

Before they left the library, they asked Esther about the Chupadera Mountains.

"They're a small volcanic range. Just south of town, west of the Rio Grande. Don't expect to see the Alps, they're pretty low, no trees to speak of, but they can be fairly rugged if you're exploring on foot."

Tully examined the claim map. "Not many landmarks." Esther shook her head. "But it looks like the claim is on the north side of Black Canyon."

"Let me help you," she said, and walked over to her desk with its computer. "Nobody makes paper maps anymore, but I have all the state's topographic maps in digital form, and I can print a copy showing Black Canyon."

Soon a large sheet emerged from a map printer. Pointing to a dotted blue line, Esther said, "That's Black

Canyon there. Unfortunately, it wiggles around all over the place—don't think Grand Canyon—but your claim is near the junction with Little Black Canyon, here. That should get you fairly close."

#

"Now what?" asked Samster as they climbed back into his mother's car.

"We have to find Toler's claims. Don't you think that would be interesting? And that might lead us to the ORO sketched on the back of the map."

"Esther said the claim was in the Chupadera Mountains, and that they're fairly close to Socorro."

"Yeah, but we don't have time on this trip to launch an expedition to the Chupaderas."

"Let's go see Crazy Tony. He'll have some ideas."

Tully frowned. "I don't know ..."

"Let's face it, we can't visit Tony when Wendy is around. Now's the time. We can ask him, in a general way, about mining in the Chupadera Mountains. Maybe he knows about dacite."

"But we're not going to mention the map, under any circumstances. Agreed?"

"Agreed."

#

Finding where Crazy Tony lived wasn't easy. They knew from earlier conversations that it was near the western edge of town, near Socorro Spring, off Garcia Street, but they had to ask directions when they found themselves in a maze of dirt roads and driveways, most unmarked, leading to a diffuse community of shacks and trailers.

After being chased away from several properties by packs of threatening dogs, they finally shouted their request to an older man in dirty overalls, who pointed them toward a trailer isolated from others in the area.

As they approached, they were halted by a cable strung between two iron posts and a hand-painted sign: "Posted. No Trespassing. This means you. Trespassers will be shot."

Before they could do anything, three large dogs charged toward them, barking, teeth bared. Behind them a man emerged from the trailer with a rifle cradled in his arms.

"Hey, Tony," Tully shouted. "It's me, Tully, and Samster."

Both the dogs and the man continued their approach. Suddenly the man stopped and barked something to the dogs, who stopped and turned to look at him. Tony kept walking toward them, the dogs now at his heels.

"Well, hello there, young fellers. I wasn't expecting company." He didn't smile as he spoke.

Tully wasn't sure how to approach him, so he went with a tried-and-true fallback strategy: flattery.

"Samster and I were in Socorro on ... research, and we were interested in the local geology and mining history, and we figured no one would know more than you."

"Mining history, eh?" He still didn't smile, but he didn't frown, which Tully took as a good sign.

"Up on the Rio Grande you proved you knew that kind of thing," Samster echoed. "You sure knew where to pan."

"But we're not here to look for gold or to do any panning," Tully added quickly. "I'm a history student, and this area had quite a mining history. We figured you'd know it."

Flattery seemed to be working.

"Well, come on to the house, and I'll fill you in. There's lots of stuff that happened here that folks don't know, that ain't in the history books." And with that he turned and walked back toward the trailer.

Crazy Tony's trailer was a weathered tri-color—turquoise, white, and rust—that time and Tony had altered with attached sheds and stove pipes and what passed for a porch; no one could imagine the trailer when it was new, any more than one could imagine Tony as a young boy. Bare sheets of tar paper were tacked onto the sides.

The trailer was the main island of an archipelago of ramshackle outbuildings, piles of junk, mounds of rocks, and rusting pieces of equipment of unknown purpose. Tony's old Ford pickup was parked beside the trailer, near two other vehicles likely used for parts. Opposite the trailer stood a wooden outhouse, a one-holer; its door hung askew on one hinge. Nearby a hand-dug pit contained charred trash, while adjacent to it were several rusty barrels heaped with aluminum beer cans. Samster nudged Tully and whispered, "Tony's savings account."

They followed Tony onto the uneven porch. "Find something to sit on," he said. Tully chose a wooden box, Samster a pile of flat rocks. Tony slouched into the porch's only chair, a rickety rocking chair of unpainted wood. Tully could not help but contrast Crazy Tony's hospitality with that of Wilbur Frost.

"So you're in town for research, and you're interested in mining history." It wasn't a question. "Well, these parts saw a lot of it. That's why the School of Mines is here. I expect you've been to the library they have."

Tully and Samster nodded. "We didn't learn much," Samster added. Tully shot him a warning glance.

Tony seemed not to have noticed but rather continued. "But them professors don't know shit about what mining's really like. You got to get down into the mines, burrow into 'em like a badger, get to know what it's like when your carbide lamp runs out of water and all you've got is your bladder and your dick."

Samster gulped.

"Yeah, and beat your head against a rock ceiling and smell the armpits and farts of everyone who's ever been in the hole before you, listened to the creaking of timbers that ain't supposed to creak—yeah, you gotta do all that and more to really call yourself a miner."

"And I thought being a bike mechanic was dirty business," said Samster.

Tony snorted his contempt.

"So where was the mining around here concentrated?" asked Tully, trying to change the subject. "The Socorro Mountains? The Magdalena Mountains? Maybe the Chupadera Mountains—they sound interesting. Do you know them?"

Almost imperceptibly Tony's eyes narrowed. "The Chupaderas, eh? Ain't many people call them interesting."

Tully smiled his boyish grin. "Maybe that's why they're interesting."

Tony let that slide. "There was a lot of activity down there in the late 1800s, the usual bunch of pilgrims swarmin' around, lookin' under every rock, but nothing much came of it. They dug out some lead and silver, but not much to speak of, and all the mines closed when the silver market collapsed. Course, that don't mean silver ain't there, waitin' to be discovered, some fabulously rich deposit like the Bridal Chamber over in Lake Valley— you've heard of that?"

Tully nodded.

Apparently not noticing Tony continued, "Yep, they hauled 2.5 million ounces of silver out of there, some of it so pure they cut it with a saw. But the man who found it was killed by Apaches on the same day of his discovery. Who's to say these treasures don't come with a curse?"

Tully noticed Samster's eyes widening.

"Now if you want to talk silver," Tony continued, "you're talking the Magdalena Mountains. You know the old town of Kelly? Now there was a silver camp ..."

An hour later, Tully took advantage of a full bladder to interrupt Tony's monologue. "Mind if I use the outhouse?"

"Help yourself."

When Tully returned, having dutifully sprinkled lime into the hole from a coffee can kept in the outhouse, he found Tony saying to Samster, "Dacite, huh? Yeah, I know dacite, a mining man can't help knowing dacite, it's a volcanic rock, and this area was once a bunch of volcanoes. It doesn't form country rock, like granite or rhyolite, but it crops up as dikes or sills. I'll show you some, I've got a piece over here."

Tully and Samster followed him as he got up and walked to a pile of rocks near a shed. He handed them a dense light-gray rock mottled with flecks of white. Tully examined it, then handed it to Samster.

Before Tully could stop him Samster asked, "Do you ever find gold in dacite?"

Tony's eyes narrowed, and he hesitated before he answered. "Well, as I said, it's volcanic and often forms dikes. No prospector worth his salt ever passes up looking at a dike, but it's not famous for being gold-bearing." Then he said, "Why do you ask?"

"Oh, no particular reason, just curiosity," replied Tully. Even to himself it sounded lame and phony.

"There's dacite around here, lots of places. If you have *something*"—he emphasized the word—"you want to check out, I'll help you. Lots of good leads get missed by people who don't know what they're looking at."

"Thanks, we may take you up on that, but right now we're not prospecting, just trying to get a feel for the area's history." Tully hoped the lie wasn't as obvious as it sounded.

Tony just nodded.

"You know, Samster," Tully said, "we've taken up too much of Tony's time already, and we need to get back to Albuquerque. Tony, thank you so much, you've been a great help, and we appreciate it."

Tony didn't speak as he walked them back to the locked gate and their car. As they climbed in he said, "You let me know about that dacite." And with that he turned and walked away.

#

"I'm sorry, Tully, I guess I just got carried away." Samster looked like a dog that had just pissed on the carpet.

"It's okay. I'd have done the same thing."

"But I think he picked up on it."

"Yeah, but we didn't mention the map. All we have to do is steer clear of Crazy Tony, and he'll forget all about us."

"Sounds logical, but why do I have the feeling Tony doesn't forget anything that smells of gold?"

#

Later that day Esther the librarian heard the door open. She looked up to see Tony entering. She frowned. Not only was it almost closing time, but Tony Kalvari was her least favorite patron. He was rude and had a reputation in town for violence. He had no interest in geology deeper than lost treasures, and more than once she'd suspected him of filching maps and articles from the library. Also, he stank. She didn't bother to greet him as he sidled up to her desk.

"I'm afraid we're closing soon," she said.

"That's okay. I've just got a few quick questions."

Her apprehension rose. Apparently his interest was not in the collections.

"I was visited by a couple of nice young fellers from Albuquerque this afternoon. They asked me to help 'em with some research they was doing, but I'm damned if it didn't all slip out of my head. They said they'd been here, so I was hoping you could refresh my memory. They was nice young fellers, and I'd like to help 'em if I could."

Esther relaxed. Tony wasn't his usual surly self today, and she might get rid of him quickly.

"Well, yes, they were here. The taller one is a doctoral student in Western history, the smaller one works at a bike shop there. They were trying to track down information on some claims on an old claim sheet they had."

"I know those old claim sheets. I hope they had better luck than I usually have getting information from them."

"They got lucky. Their particular claim was one Dick Everly inventoried."

"Now, that's interesting. Do remember which claim it was? I know a lot of those old claims, and I'd sure like to help them young fellers, if I could."

Esther frowned. Tony wasn't exactly known around Socorro for being helpful to anyone. "Oh, it wasn't much, just some obscure claim from the 1880s in the Chupaderas. Guy that filed the claim didn't really work it, so I doubt it amounted to anything. That's all I remember. You're welcome to look in the Everly files, but as you know there were hundreds of minor claims in the Chupaderas." She hoped that would get rid of Tony, as he was only marginally literate and certainly not one to spend hours reading old reports.

"The Chupaderas, eh?" Tony's eyes narrowed. "That's odd, them mountains didn't really amount to anything for mining."

"As I said, one of the young men is a history student at the university, and I think the other was just a friend. They weren't really mining or prospector types. His dissertation could be something completely unrelated too the actual value of the mines."

Tony continued looking puzzled, then abruptly he turned and left the library. He didn't thank Esther for her help.

#

Tony's characteristic scowl deepened as he strode across campus from the library. He hated the university, hated the professors, hated the students. They represented everything he wasn't: with money, privileged, educated, with bright futures. He'd spent his whole life down and out and dirty, knocking around the West, chasing one false hope after another, only to be finally cast up on the shores of this wretched town.

And now he hated the two young men from Albuquerque. The taller one a history student. The shorter one didn't look like a university type, but he still was young, with a future.

Tony hated going onto the Albuquerque campus, felt out-of-place, inferior, but a bike shop, shouldn't be hard to find someone at a bike shop.

And if those two had somehow come across clues to a gold deposit ...

He gritted his teeth at the unfairness of it. Not once, in a lifetime of searching, had any of the myriad maps and clues and rumors and miners' tales led him to anything more than fool's gold and hard times. If anyone was owed a genuine strike, it was him. He'd jumped claims before; if those two had something genuine, he'd get it, one way or another. He was owed. He wouldn't be cheated out of what was due.

CHAPTER 12

Students were spewing out the front door of the Happy Jelly Bean Preschool when Tully arrived. Mothers and a few men waited by the curb. When the flow subsided Tully entered and went to Wendy's room. The colorful construction paper cutouts of plants and animals, the bright posters with enthusiastic messages, the sunny smiley faces pasted to student papers tacked to a bulletin board—all were in harsh contrast to Wendy's face.

Her hair hung in strings, her mouth sagged, and her eyes were dark and tired. She didn't say anything when he entered but just looked up from righting the chairs that had been upended around a low table.

"Bad day, huh," said Tully then immediately regretted the inanity of his observation.

When she still didn't say anything, he said, "Anything particularly bad happen?"

"Oh, just the usual tears, tantrums, psychotic episodes—oh, and the boys had another piss-off in the bathroom. Just the usual."

"I'm sorry. Hey, you want to go to Starbuck's, get some coffee, maybe meet up with Samster, relax, take your mind off things?"

She straightened up, put her hands on her hips. "You just don't get it, do you?"

"Huh?"

She shook her head in disgust. "I thought we had an understanding that we did things together."

"We do," Tully protested. "That's what I was suggesting."

"So you go sneaking off with Samster to Socorro to do something you know I won't approve of."

"It wasn't exactly sneaking off ..."

"Bullshit! Can you deny you'd have preferred I didn't know about it? Neither of you is a skilled conspirator."

Tully's eyebrows raised in a question. Wendy continued. "I stopped by the library to see you, and they told me you'd gone off with Samster, then I went to the Honors Center to see Peggy, and she told me."

Tully shuffled his feet. "I'd have told you, sooner or later."

Wendy shook her head and went back to picking up chairs.

"Look, Wendy, you're right, going alone with Samster avoided some potential unpleasantness between you and me. That's a shitty excuse. You have every right to be pissed at me. But you also have to know that this doesn't threaten my commitment to you or to finishing my dissertation. This is just a hobby, nothing more."

Then his face brightened. "You know those letters on the map? QTQ? Elron figured out that they're a code. When you decipher it, it spells *ORO*–gold. That map is a treasure map!!"

Wendy's mouth dropped open. Then, stammering in outrage, she said, "You took off from your research here to drive to Socorro to research a supposed treasure map! And did you find it, a pot of gold? Or nuggets just lying on the ground?"

"I don't really believe there's any gold, and Crazy Tony didn't say anything to persuade me otherwise."

She boggled again. "Crazy Tony! You two went and saw Crazy Tony?"

Tully shrank two inches. "It was all just geology. We didn't say anything to him about the map, or the ORO."

"Crazy Freaking Tony? I'd almost rather you went there for an assignation with a crack whore than that ... that ... He's not just crazy, he's evil."

"That's a bit strong. I admit he's probably not the most scrupulous person around, but ..."

"Look, I never want to tell you who you can associate with and who you can't, but nothing good will come from hanging around that man."

Tully attempted a laugh. "You don't have to worry. Tony didn't exactly put out the welcome mat for us."

"I don't want to hear about it."

"You're right. Your objections are well taken. And speaking of doing things together, will you still go with me to the departmental party tonight? I know we're kind of shaky right now, but I'd really appreciate it. You could meet some of the people in the department."

"Will Elnora be there?"

Tully nodded.

"Yeah, I can go. They'll be better company than Crazy Tony."

Tully laughed. "I wouldn't be too sure about that."

#

Wendy saw Samster sitting alone in the student union building, with a cup of tea and the campus newspaper. He looked up as she stood before him. Again her hands rested on her hips.

"So you and Tully sneaked off to Socorro to go chasing after that ORO nonsense?"

She skewered Samster with her gaze. He had never before faced her wrath. They were friends, close friends, and she wasn't sure how he'd react to her anger, despite knowing it was directed more at Tully than him.

"We didn't exactly 'sneak off.' It was more like a strategic maneuver. We knew you wouldn't have approved, so we spared you the dilemma of deciding whether or not to go along."

"That's just what Tully said. Did you rehearse your stories for me?"

"Honest, we weren't being sneaky, at least not as in 'sneaky.' If you'd asked, we'd have told you."

"How noble of you. But you were right: I don't approve. And you know why. He's got to get serious about his dissertation or his academic career will crash. And you *know* that."

Samster looked down at his feet. "I do know that. I reminded him of that as we drove down."

"And what did he say?"

"He said this wouldn't jeopardize his commitment to you or his career."

"And? ..."

"I reminded him that I wouldn't know much about those things, not having either a girlfriend or a career."

Wendy's anger dissolved. "Oh, Samster, I don't mean to be angry with you. Tully, yes, but not you."

"Why not me? Is it because I don't have anything to lose chasing ghosts? Everyone's looking after Tully, but no one's looking after me because ... hell, I'm just a stoner bicycle mechanic. Who cares if I blow off my life?"

Impulsively she threw her arms around him. "Oh, Samster, you're not just that, not to me."

When she released him he said, "I know. And you're not just a kid-herder to me." He smiled a sheepish smile. "But let's face it, if we found a rich gold mine, or stolen bank loot, and suddenly became rich, all our career prospects definitely would improve."

Not wishing to push the issue Wendy just rolled her eyes. "I hope our dreams don't depend on rocks and bank loot."

CHAPTER 13

Elnora loathed departmental parties. The day should have been over; she should be heading home to her cats, to her fireplace, to her stereo programmed for appropriate relaxing-at-home classical music. Instead she was walking into the university's faculty club for the worst of all abominations, a departmental party. At these gatherings, interactions were artificial, always unsteady as to where or where not to go, and it only got worse when alcohol was involved.

Spencer loved these parties. With a few, or several, drinks in him, his wit and charm and bonhomie coruscated—until inevitably they didn't.

He was charming now. "Good evening, Elnora, so glad you could make it." As department chair it was Spencer's role to greet arrivals, so she expected to see him. The sarcasm in his voice was far beneath detection by most people who didn't know him, and though he held his signature glass of bourbon the evening was too young for any egregious slurring of his words.

"I wouldn't miss it," Elnora said, as sincerely as she could. She smiled warmly at the small, middle-aged woman standing beside Spencer. "Even though it's a bittersweet occasion."

Helen Mobley, the latest of many department secretaries, was leaving for better pay elsewhere. Elnora mouthed platitudes about being sorry to see Helen go, then entered the room that already was crowded with people and thick with small talk. She made her way to the bar, where she ordered a glass of white wine. Next she heaped a plate with hors d'oeuvres. She hoped both would last the evening. She then she scanned for people with whom to pass time as pleasantly as possible. She headed for Tully and Wendy.

"Pretty good turnout," effused Tully. He wore khaki slacks that almost went with his Harris tweed jacket with the leather elbow patches. Beneath he wore a maroon turtleneck. She'd seen the outfit before; he wore it to every formal occasion. It looked like it was the only non-casual outfit he owned—and indeed it was. It made him appear like a hippie trying to pass for professorial, but the outfit went well with his characteristic bright, open smile.

Wendy wore a graceful beige skirt, topped by a blue-and-gold sash of some oriental pedigree. The two complemented her white silk blouse. Tasteful and restrained, just like her smile.

"Good to see you," said Wendy. "I don't know most of these people."

"And unfortunately I do."

Wendy raised her eyebrows.

"Sorry, just kidding. There are some delightful people here, and Tully and I can introduce you to them. That tiny woman over there? That's Dorothy Liggon. She can enter a Modern History conference and make half the people there tremble in fear that she won't approve of what they say. She's a charming person.

"And that young man talking to her is Toby Torrez, an assistant professor in Spanish colonial missions. He's charming too, but be careful, unless you have a burning desire to know *everything* about Spanish missions."

Tully laughed. "He really is a nice guy."

Then Elnora's eyes fell upon Spencer, who had moved from the entrance to the bar. Tully and Elnora glanced at each other.

"I suppose you should meet him," said Elnora to Wendy, "but make it sooner rather than later." She watched as Spencer refilled his glass.

Wendy looked at Tully, who nodded.

"Thanks for the advice. Tully, perhaps we should go over there now."

But before they reached Spencer, they greeted Toby Torrez, and Wendy let slip that her dream was to photograph old churches in New Mexico. Half an hour later, bearing a napkin list of must-see sites, they left him and made their way toward the bar, where Spencer leaned against it and appeared to be lecturing to a young, female grad student.

"Ah, Tully," exclaimed Spencer grandly as Tully and Wendy arrived. "Bartender, kindly refill their glasses—and mine—that this occasion not go uncelebrated with unctuous spirits."

Wendy reluctantly allowed her wine glass to be topped off, while Tully, considerably less reluctantly, allowed his glass to be refilled with what Wendy saw was an unknown species of bourbon. He tasted it, then grimaced.

"Unaccustomed to spirits of such nobility, eh?" Spencer guffawed. "I'm afraid we don't have any bean vodka!" He guffawed again.

Tully took another taste, and managed to keep his face straight.

Spencer turned to Wendy. "I don't believe I've had the pleasure of meeting this young lady." When Wendy extended her hand, he took it and kissed it. Wendy made a face like she'd just found a maggot in her drink.

But Spencer had already returned his attention to the female grad student. "Tully, this is Allison, an addition to our graduate program in American history." Spencer took a swallow of his drink, which Tully matched, as if on a dare. Wendy gave Allison a smile she hoped conveyed understanding and sympathy.

"And Tully, here, is our department's expert on beans."

Tully took another swallow of his drink and said, "There's more to beans than meets the eye."

"Or the nose," snarked Spencer.

Tully started to say something, but he felt a gentle but insistent nudge in the ribs from Wendy.

"Actually, Tully's main interest is in things that don't exist," Spencer continued. Tully's eyebrows knitted into a frown. Allison raised her eyes questioningly.

"Yes, Tully's quite the authority on the West's great mining discoveries that never happened."

Tully reddened as he turned to Allison. "He means legends of lost mines, and it's true that most of them never existed, but that doesn't mean the legends don't have historical significance as folklore."

"And word around the department is that you've even uncovered a lost bean mine, and you're looking for that," Spencer continued.

Elnora, aware that tensions and voices were rising, joined the people at the bar.

"Dammit," said Tully, "you're misrepresenting everything. Legends were important in the West." Wendy noticed that

Tully had begun to slur his words."

Spencer chortled. Then seeing Elnora, he said, "Speaking of legends, here's Hardrock Elnora Atkins. She has her own will-o'-the-wisps she's chasing. Perhaps we should call ourselves the Department of Pseudo-History."

"That's quite enough, Spencer," Elnora stated in a low voice that in anyone but Spencer would have induced sobriety.

Instead he charged ahead. "Come on, everyone knows Tully is an incurable, woolly-headed romantic, and you're not much better with—who is it, Ragtime Annie?"

Sloshing his drink Tully leaned into Spencer's face and shouted, "And everyone knows you're an asshole. You hear me, an asshole!"

Spencer paled, but before he could respond Wendy firmly grasped Tully's arm. "That's enough, we're leaving." And she all but dragged him toward the door.

Someone in the room attempted applause, but the rage on Spencer's face aborted it.

For the first time in anyone's memory he could only splutter, and just as he started to find words someone said loudly, "A toast! A toast for Helen Mobley!"

"Hear! Hear!" said Dorothy Liggon in the loudest voice anyone had ever heard from her. Glasses were raised, and someone tactfully demanded that Helen say a few words.

The crisis had passed.

The next afternoon Tully schlumped on the couch in his apartment, sipping a cup of tea. Two days ago it would have been a glass of wine, but he wasn't ready to make up with alcohol right now. Besides, it would detract from the satisfaction he felt. Withal it had been a good day. The blowback from his gaffe at the party had been minimal. If anything, it had raised his status in the department.

The phone rang. Elnora.

"Tully, I don't like making this call, but I'm afraid I underestimated Spencer's vindictiveness toward you."

Tully waited.

"This afternoon he sent around a memo to the faculty saying the department needed to become more efficient. It said some students were taking too long getting their degrees and clogging the process. He didn't mention you by name, but the implication was pretty clear, I'm afraid."

"Clogging the process—yeah, that would be me."

"He proposed setting deadlines, and candidates who don't meet them will be dropped. He proposed a four-year limit on dissertation completion ..."

Tully gasped. He'd already burned three of those years.

"It still has to be approved by the full faculty, but the deadline isn't entirely unreasonable, and I suspect there'll be enough support for it to pass. A few other departments on campus have adopted similar rules."

Tully sighed. "Okay. That gives me a year. Well, you have said most doctoral candidates wind up working around the clock, and I guess my time has come."

"It has, Tully. But you can do it. *We* can do it. You have my complete support."

When he hung up, his swagger faltered. One year—and he'd barely started. For three years he'd just farted around, doing other things. He doubted Elnora fully understood how little he'd accomplished. Now he had to accomplish four years' work in one. He wasn't sure he could do it. He'd never been a disciplined researcher. He recalled the term papers—the majority—that he'd written the night before deadline. Some he'd slid beneath the instructor's door at the end of the day. Once he'd even used the "my dog ate my homework" line. Unfortunately it was true; the instructor was acquainted with Howdy and accepted the excuse.

But that wouldn't work with a doctoral dissertation. And he'd hoped that for once he'd do it right, pace himself, produce something he could be proud of, something that would advance his career.

Now he had a year.

For the first time he confronted what being booted from the department would mean. All his life he'd just assumed he'd be able to slide by on his intellect and charm and that opportunities would open for him. It had worked in high school, and in his graduate classes. But a dissertation was different. He couldn't throw something together at the last minute.

He'd leave the department in disgrace. His fellow graduate students would view him with smug pity. Sure, there'd be talk about coming back and finishing later, but no one ever did. He'd have to find another career–but what? A librarian? Working in the library part-time was okay as a student but as his life's work? The tedium and bureaucracy would consume his soul. If he didn't want to just shelve books he'd have to get a degree in library science. Compared to that researching beans looked positively thrilling. Work in a bookstore, like other failed Humanities students?

As he reviewed the options he realized with horror that he'd spend the rest of his life asking, "What if?"

And Wendy? He was confident she'd stick with him wherever his career path took him, but she'd be married to someone bitter and perpetually angry with himself.

What should he tell Wendy now? And *should* he tell Wendy? He didn't want to deceive or mislead her, and he trusted her not to rag on him—too much. But the fact that he'd put himself in this position would diminish him in her eyes.

There was a chance, a slight chance, that he could pull it off. He'd begin now. He went into his bedroom and began organizing his desk.

CHAPTER 14

Wendy maintained a frosty reserve between herself and Tully as they drove to Pleasant Valley. This was a research trip to Bean Country, yes, Tully said again and again, a research trip, to further his dissertation. To Wendy, Tully was like a puppy, crushed when reprimanded then wagging his tail and happy again when the moment passed. And as with a puppy she found it very difficult to remain angry with him. He had been the one to suggest they stop near an abandoned homesteader cabin so she could take photos. He even had pointed out details and angles other people would miss.

Tully. Was her love was fading? No, she loved Tully as much as ever, but forgiving him was becoming more difficult.

#

The streets of Pleasant Valley—no, make that "street"—were empty of life. Wendy sat in the car and waited as Tully knocked on doors, hoping to find someone who could give him personal reminiscences of life in Bean Country. Now she watched him approach the car with his long, loping stride, disappointment on his face.

"There was an old gray cat I had a good conversation with," he said sourly as he climbed in the car, "but she kept reminding me that beans weren't her thing. I left a few notes in mailboxes asking people to call me. I didn't bother including my email address. This just isn't an email sort of place."

"Sorry."

"That's okay. Actually, I did catch a few people at home, but they didn't know much. The cat was more forthcoming. One old guy became positively belligerent when I asked him about the salt lakes area."

Wendy frowned. "And why were you asking about the salt lakes? You're not pursuing that Lost Pinto Treasure, are you?" She'd noticed that Tully and Samster had begun using that term to refer to Oscar Bollinger's hidden bank money.

"Pursuing is too strong a word. I just find it interesting, and despite what everyone says, it is a part of local culture. Besides, it's not like I'm giving up important research to ask a question or two."

Wendy shook her head.

"And along those lines," Tully continued, "we're still got a few hours of daylight left, let's take a spin out to the salt lakes."

Wendy's eyes widened, her frown deepened.

Tully pushed on. "We're not doing anything else, and the salt lakes did figure in the economic history here. They're all that remains of the great Pleistocene lake that created the bean-growing soil here. And, trust me on this, I don't want to go there to look for the Lost Pinto Treasure. Hell, I wouldn't know where to begin looking."

She tried a diversion. "We could visit Wilbur Frost?"

"Just as soon not," Tully said. Clearly he remembered the

harsh treatment he'd received the last time they'd visited the old homesteader.

Wendy was silent a moment. They really had struck out for the day, nothing left to do, and Tully had indulged her photography. A quick trip to the salt lakes might even quell his interest in the missing bank loot legend.

"Okay. Maybe the salt lakes will be interesting, photographically."

#

The sun was about two hours from setting when a rough two-track led them to a faint cattle trail leading down a broad wash toward one of the salt lakes, about a mile distant. They were late in arriving, as they'd taken several wrong turns on unmarked dirt roads, with no one to ask directions. They had driven by Wilbur Frost's place but decided not to stop.

Perhaps the lateness was a good thing, thought Wendy. She really hadn't wanted to see the old homesteader either. And besides, the late afternoon light was great for photography. As Wendy unloaded her camera equipment she could see the salt-encrusted cliffs encircling the lake turning a pale gold.

"I'll help you with that," said Tully, as he hoisted a tripod over his shoulder and began down the slope.

Not a single tree, Wendy noticed as she walked, and even the grasses and shrubs were having a hard time of it. Tough, gnarly sacaton, snakeweed, gray tough grass–all bent over by an insistent late-afternoon wind. Where the plants had given up a white alkali crust had formed on the bare soil. Here and there were a few dried cow pies. How many acres would it take to feed one cow, she wondered? And as for growing crops here, where even the native plants could barely survive ...

Wendy found the solitude of the place oppressive, even slightly creepy. She recalled Wilbur Frost describing how after Oscar Bollinger had disappeared kids would keep an eye out for his body, horror mingled with excitement. They'd never found anything, and she reassured herself that this area, so close to his homestead, surely had been thoroughly searched.

The light was deepening further, the breeze stiffening, when they arrived at the lake. Wendy could see a skiff of shallow water toward the basin's center, tiny waves on its surface. She knew that once the entire valley had been a real lake. Paleo-Indians had fished from its shores. Then the climate went dry, water departed, leaving behind its dissolved minerals and a few pathetic puddles like this. All this she knew from Tully's travelogue as they'd driven here.

She began setting up her tripod while Tully loped across the flats to a nearby cliff.

Suddenly Tully stopped, followed immediately by what sounded like a rifle shot.

Tully ran back to her. Just as he reached her she heard a whining sound over head, again followed immediately by another rifle report.

"Hey!" Tully shouted. "Don't shoot in this direction. We're down here."

As if to answer another shot sounded. Less than three feet away dust exploded.

"That's no hunter!" Tully shouted. "He's shooting at *us!*"

Seizing Wendy's arm he dragged her, still clutching her tripod, to the lee of a sand dune.

Wendy, who never before had been shot at, was paralyzed by fear. Her instinct was to burrow deeper into the sand dune, to vanish.

"What's going on?" she gasped.

"I don't know. Someone's shooting at us." Another bullet skimmed the dune's top. "I think he's shooting from above the cliffs.

"We've got to move before he does," said Tully. "He could be going around behind us right now. Come on."

Despite her terror, Wendy followed Tully as he scuttled crab-like along the dune's base.

Tully nodded to his right. "If we can get to that arroyo we can follow it up and stay out of sight."

Though Wendy's instinct still was to huddle motionless, she could not avoid the logic of Tully's plan.

But to reach the arroyo they would have to leave the dunes for a twenty-five-yard dash to the arroyo's mouth. They paused. Then Tully said, "You go first, he'll shoot at me when he realizes what we're doing. Let's go." Wendy took a deep breath and sprinted toward the arroyo. Tully followed.

The adrenaline surge eased some of Wendy's terror, and with a strange detachment she found herself wondering, even as she pushed her body, what it would feel like to be shot.

Almost as if in answer the hidden assailant fired another round. It struck in the sand behind Tully. She raced even faster. Just as she and Tully dived into the arroyo another shot came, again landing just behind them.

They raced up the arroyo, tripping over boulders and deadwood.

The arroyo fed into the salt lake, and following it upstream would lead away from the lake and the shooter, though when it ended at its head they would be exposed on the barren plains.

As the arroyo rose and narrowed, they could see their car a quarter of a mile away. The salt lake and the shooter were at least that far behind them. "We have to run for it," said Tully.

Let's start together but split up and zig-zag, to make a more difficult target." Wendy couldn't believe she'd actually said that, but she realized anger was giving her lucidity where fear had not.

Tully nodded, then said, "Now!"

They bolted from the arroyo and ran erratic separate courses to their car. A bullet whined over their heads.

Tully gulped lungfuls of air when he reached the safe side of the car, just seconds ahead of Wendy. He opened the door to the passenger side and wriggled in. Wendy followed. Then keeping as low as possible he put the key in the ignition. To actually start the car he had to depress the clutch while the engine cranked, requiring him to sit up. In the interminable time it took for the engine to catch, Wendy expected the drive-side window to shatter. Would the car's body stop a bullet? Unless it hit the frame, probably not.

When the engine finally caught, Tully slammed the car into gear and floored the accelerator, churning up rooster tails of dust as the car sped away.

#

"Whoa!" exclaimed Tully when he caught his breath. "What was *that* all about?"

Wendy struggled to regain normal breathing. Between gasps she said, "That wasn't some near-sighted hunter mistaking us for antelope. Whoever he was he was shooting at *us*."

"He was indeed," said Tully. "But I don't think he wanted to kill us so much as scare us." As fear ebbed, rationality returned. Wendy looked at him questioningly.

"If he'd wanted to kill us," Tully continued, "he'd have waited until we got closer. We were moving in his direction when the first shot was fired. And he fired, what, eight shots? You'd think one of them would have hit if he'd been aiming to hit us."

"If he wanted to scare us he sure succeeded. I've never been so scared in my life. Someone shooting at *me*, deliberately, consciously, with premeditation, at *me*. Oh, and you too."

"Thanks, I didn't want to be left out."

Finally breathing normally Wendy said, "But you're right. Each shot missed us by the same distance, as if the shooter was aiming a set distance away from his presumed target."

Wendy shuddered. *Shooter* and *target* were two words she never wanted to hear in reference to herself.

"That bastard!" Wendy's slammed her hand on the steering wheel. "Just who the hell does he think he is that he can go around shooting at innocent people, scaring the daylights out of them?"

Wendy seethed, anger replacing fear. Someone shooting at *them*—it was an outrage! If the shooter had wanted them to get off private land, he could have just come down and told them to leave, and they'd have done it! There simply was no need to scare them half to death, to send them scurrying back to the car like a couple of frightened rabbits. That bastard!

#

All the way back to Albuquerque Tully and Wendy discussed the incident. "We should go back and look for the shooter's tracks," said Tully. "I think I know about where he would have been."

Wendy humphed. "Great, you go first and give me a report. I'm not ashamed to admit I was terrified. We should inform the sheriff that someone in his county is taking pot shots at innocent strangers."

"No, we should not report this to the authorities. After all, we weren't exactly 'innocent.' We were trespassing on private land. In rural New Mexico, that's justifiable reason to shoot at strangers."

Wendy sat silently. Then she said, "Someone knew we were going there. Who could that be?"

"Beats me. Could be anyone. We weren't exactly sneaky about going out there. It could have been someone in Pleasant Valley who saw us heading that way. Hell, for all I know it was that old codger who was so irascible when I asked about the salt lakes. Or maybe it was someone who didn't know about us at all, who just happened to be there and wanted to scare away some outsiders."

"But why? There's *nothing* there. No cattle to rustle, no old homes to vandalize, nothing to steal. Just some miserable land no one has ever had any use for. Why would anyone want to terrorize ordinary *innocent* people without even asking them what they were doing? Why?"

Tully's pursed his lips, knitted his eyebrows. "Maybe some ornery kid out hunting rabbits who decided to have a little fun with his gun. Maybe some militant property-rights advocate who doesn't care if the land is worthless." He chuckled. "Maybe the ghost of Oscar Bollinger still protecting his hidden bank loot."

"That's not funny," said Wendy.

CHAPTER 15

Tully and Samster sat at the table in Tully's apartment, a half-empty pizza box between them, an empty six-pack of Heineken's beer beside it.

"So Wendy was really pissed about the Lost Pinto Treasure thing?" Samster said as he pulled a slice from the box and took it to the microwave. The pizza was just as good as it had been the day before.

"She was—and I don't blame her. She deserves better. That whole thing about that farmer having bunch of cash hidden away in some caves is just bullshit. For one thing, those bills would be moldy, rotten, and rodent-gnawed by now. For another, if he had all that money, why'd he live such a hardscrabble life? That's always been the great fallacy of so many lost mine stories, especially the Lost Dutchman."

\#

After Samster left, Tully reflected on the Lost Dutchman Mine. He had mixed feelings about debunking the legend to Samster. A part of him enjoyed the debunking; the more he knew about the legends the easier debunking them became. He knew that Samster considered him the ultimate authority.

But at the same time Tully felt hypocritical, for he was far more enthralled with the legends than Samster, who after all was innocent. Tully knew the fallacies and flaws and clichés, yet he was as defenseless as Samster before the allure of the old map with ORO scribbled on it.

Adolescent. Long ago he should have outgrown his fascination with lost treasures, yet he hadn't. Nor was it merely a casual interest, a hobby—for heaven's sake he was about to lose his girlfriend and his career over lost treasures. He epitomized what Joseph Conrad had said "There is no getting away from a treasure that once fastens upon your mind. A man will curse the day he ever heard of it, but he will never forget it until he is dead." Did that mean he was doomed to die still searching for treasures he knew with almost certainty did not exist?

Was it any wonder Wendy was becoming fed up with him? She deserved better than a life married to a half-crazy treasure hunter. But what part of himself would he sacrifice if he abandoned lost treasures?

#

Samster also pondered the Lost Pinto story as he rode his bicycle from Tully's apartment. Sure, the odds were slim of someone finding the hidden bank loot, but what a payoff! Opening his own bike shop. Sending Elron to college, allowing his mother to work on her ceramics in a house without a mortgage and boarders.

He was still savoring the fantasy as he pulled into the driveway of the small home near the university that he shared with his mother and Elron. When Samster's father took off long ago, the house he left behind was part of his legacy of good riddance. It was on a corner lot on the fringe of the "student ghetto," which made for some interesting Friday nights but allowed Peggy and him to walk to work, avoiding the expense of owning a car. The house was cramped for three adults, but they got by. They had converted a semi-attached garage into an apartment.

As Samster wheeled up to the driveway, he immediately noticed Richard's car parked with its back to the garage and Richard loading boxes into the trunk. Samster nodded a perfunctory greeting; Richard glared in return.

"What's up with Richard," asked Samster as he entered the kitchen, where Peggy and Elron sat at a crude wooden table, another craft fair souvenir.

Her mouth set in a fierce grimace, Peggy said, "Richard won't be living here any more." Then she got up and stormed out of the room.

Samster's raised eyebrows questioned Elron.

"Richard spent a little too much time this afternoon with his friend, Budweiser, who encouraged him to make the very, very bad decision to make an inappropriate advance to our mother."

"That son of a bitch." Samster started to rise from the table.

"Sit down. It's already taken care off. If you look closely at Richard's face you can see a red palm print that matches perfectly Mom's right hand."

Grudgingly Samster lowered himself back into his seat.

"Then she gave him his walking papers. Said she wanted him out by sundown. That's what he's doing now, moving out."

"I'm sorry it took something like this to get rid of that jerk, but at least he's going."

"Yeah, he's going, walking away from three months unpaid rent and an apartment that's unrentable without major repairs. Mom's furious. She needs the rent to pay for the repairs, but she can't rent it until it's fixed up. She's in real bind."

Samster ground his teeth. Much as he wanted to go out and wring cash out of Richard's worthless hide, he knew he wouldn't get much, and the confrontation would diminish the satisfaction of just having him gone.

The family needed money. Mom already was working full-time at the university, and at the most recent craft fairs she'd barely made enough to cover her booth fee.

Elron brought in spending money working on his friends' computers, but he was still stuck on the bottom rung of the high school economic ladder. His friends who worked at McDonald's made more.

That left him. He could ask Wally if he could work more hours at the bike shop, but that couldn't begin to raise the money the family needed. All three of them had made a bargain with life, that if they could do the things they enjoyed, they'd accept a life of simple poverty. It had worked until life, in the form of Richard, had broken its side of the agreement.

#

For the next several days Tully secluded himself in the university library, determined to make progress on his dissertation. Wendy didn't call, and he didn't call her. He did tell Samster about Spencer's memo and the urgency of his research.

He'd found more materials than he'd expected in the university library's local history collection. They'd been there all along; he just hadn't bothered to look for them. Now he was desperately making up for lost time.

Pinto beans. Once they'd been more important to the economy of the Estancia Valley than gold had been to New Mexico's mining camps.

And the psychology of the bean farmers hadn't been much different from that of the miners. The lure of riches from a bumper crop of beans was so great that they were willing to risk all on a good year. Not very different from miners sinking everything into a promising hole.

CHAPTER 16

Tully and Samster had sworn each other to utmost secrecy. Wendy never was to know that while she was teaching at the preschool, they would be prospecting.

"I really hate doing this," Tully said as he steered his mother's aging Tercel off the paved highway south of Socorro and onto a dirt road winding among the low hills, deep canyons, and rocky ridges of the northern Chupadera Mountains. The shadows cast by towering rounded rhyolite formations had shrunk in the midday sun, and even in spring the air was shimmering hot.

"If I was in Albuquerque I wouldn't be doing research right now," Tully continued, "I'd be sacked out in my apartment. This is a good use of time." Using the information from Esther at the library, they'd prepared a map showing the likely location of Lester Toler's claim. Some things simply could not wait.

Samster, uncharacteristically silent, nodded glumly. Tully knew that Samster's friendship with Wendy was among the few things his devil-may-care friend took very seriously.

"We don't have to actually lie to her," Tully continued. "We'll just not mention it." Samster shot him a grim, sarcastic glance that said, "Yeah, sure."

"Okay, I admit that's bullshit," Tully said. "Sometime we'll have to come clean and tell her about this, but with luck that'll be after we've found the gold."

That yielded a brief chuckle.

"And we're done with Crazy Tony, agreed?" Tully persisted. Samster only nodded.

Tully was in full rationalization mode as the car bounced along the dirt road. Sometime, perhaps soon, he'd tell Wendy. He really didn't want to deceive her. And besides, when he returned later in the day from this trip, before his date with Wendy, he'd go straight to the library and put in as much time on his dissertation as if he'd stayed in Albuquerque.

He glanced at Samster. Why did his friend appear to feel worse about deceiving Wendy than he did? What did that say about him?

This had better be worth it.

#

"We'll pull over anywhere here. We've reached Black Canyon," said Tully. He steered the car onto a rocky shoulder. The ground was barren, badly overgrazed, the only trees scattered junipers.

"Some mountains," said Samster. Ahead a shallow draw ascended west between low hills toward rocky ridges.

"Some canyon," said Tully. "Esther said not to expect the Grand Canyon. Maybe it gets more canyon-esque among those ridges."

After half a mile the canyon narrowed and deepened. They agreed that Tully would hike the canyon's dry, rocky bottom, while Samster would hike along its rim, weaving among cholla and prickly-pear cacti. Prospecting here would have been easy as little soil concealed the underlying rock formations.

The sun was directly overhead as they hiked. Slowly they picked their way up the shallow draw, stopping frequently to examine rocks and outcrops. "Here's something," Samster shouted. Tully scrambled up to find his friend standing over a shallow depression, less than six feet in diameter and three feet deep.

"That definitely is a prospect pit," said Tully, "but I don't think it's Toler's."

"Why not?"

"Too small. Whoever dug this gave up after barely scratching the surface. Toler wouldn't bother registering something as insignificant as this. But it does mean people were prospecting here."

They continued up the canyon, finding more prospect pits, some larger than others. They stopped often to drink as the heat intensified. "Prospecting's tough work," quipped Samster.

"Yeah, and we haven't even done any digging."

Near the canyon's head, just as they were about to turn back, they encountered a pit slightly larger than the others. Sitting on its rim they stared into a rubble-filled hole about twelve feet across, six feet deep, surrounded by a lip of discarded rocks.

"This could be it," Tully said. "Someone put in hard work here—and I can see why."

He walked away from the hole and picked up a rock. It was gray, with a faint purple cast. He handed it to Samster, who said skeptically, "This is what we've been walking over all along this ridge."

"Right, it's what miners call country rock, but now look at the hole." Along one side was a vein of anomalous rock, stained yellow and orange. "A solution of dissolved minerals came up along a crack here and deposited other minerals, which are lacking in that country rock. The rust color says iron was deposited, and if iron was, then maybe other metals as well."

Samster's eyes widened. He picked up pieces of the red-orange rock that had fallen into the hole.

"So there could be gold in here?"

"Probably not, or not very much. Otherwise the prospector who dug this hole wouldn't have given up on it, but he might have taken the trouble to register this as a claim—just in case."

Samster continued poking around in the hole, picking up one rock after another. Tully joined him in the hole. "Look at this," said Samster, handing Tully a pale-gray rock. "It's different from the country rock too, but it doesn't have the staining of the vein."

Tully examined it closely. Then he took a magnifying glass from his pocket. "You're right, this rock didn't come from around here. I think it's dacite—and I don't think there's much dacite in the Chupaderas." He handed the glass to Samster. "Look closely, there are tiny grains of metal in there. Probably pyrite, better known as fool's gold. It's pretty common, but it is a sign of mineralization."

Samster's eyes widened as he peered at the rock through the glass. He put the rock in his backpack.

"Look for other pieces of this," said Tully, but after an hour they had found nothing. Finally, with one last glance around the hole they started back down.

#

"Shit!" Back at the car Tully turned the key in the ignition switch. Only a click. "Gawdammit, we somehow turned the lights on, and now the battery's dead."

"Great place for it to happen," said Samster. "Let me guess, your Mom doesn't carry AAA–or a spare water container."

Tully frowned at him.

"Sorry," said Samster, "nothing personal. I guess we just wait until someone comes along who might have jumper cables."

#

They waited. They waited as they drained the last liquid from their water bottles. They waited as the sun declined in the west and shadows lengthened. They waited as the road remained empty of vehicles.

"Damn," said Tully. "I was going to go to the library and then get together with Wendy tonight. I'm toast. I'll bet karma had a hand in this. This wouldn't have happened if we'd been more up-front with Wendy. We deserve this." He kicked a stone on the road.

Samster only nodded grimly. With a deep sigh he took the rock specimen from his backpack. He turned it over and over in his hands, hoping to catch a glint of metal.

Where had this come from? He gazed at the dark outlines of mountains whose canyon they had explored. "Do you suppose these could be the mountains shown on the map?"

"I doubt it. The outline doesn't match. The Chupaderas are rounded, the map shows jagged peaks."

Samster nodded. He gazed at the darkening outlines of distant ranges, many with jagged peaks. Somewhere out there were other rocks like this, somewhere ...

Samster's reverie was interrupted when suddenly, to the south, headlights appeared. A vehicle was approaching over the dirt road. They waited until it got closer.

Soon an old pickup rattled toward them, with only the driver in the cab. Tully and Samster stood in the road and waved their arms. The truck groaned to a halt.

"The battery in our car died, can you help us? Please," Tully pleaded.

The man scrutinized them. He appeared to be in his sixties; he wore brown work pants and a dirty denim shirt, with a weathered ball cap on his head. He had a scruffy gray beard.

Samster stood nearby trying to look needy and pathetic.

"I got jumper cables in the back here, wouldn't think of traveling without 'em." He looked contemptuously at Tully.

"It's my mother's car," said Tully defensively.

The man positioned the truck so its nose faced that of Tully's car, then they popped the hoods on their vehicles. He attached the cables while Tully climbed into his car.

"Okay, try 'er now," said the man.

Tully's car's ignition grinded, then the engine caught. Samster and Tully both broke into big smiles.

"Thanks," said Tully. "Thanks a lot. I don't know what we'd have done if you hadn't come along."

"Most likely you'd have gotten to know the night sky real well," the man grunted as he tossed the cables back into the truck's bed. "If I'm out alone in this emptiness, I always have a spare battery with me. Never know what's going to happen."

"Don't we know," said Samster.

Then the man drove off.

Samster and Tully climbed into their car and followed him down the road.

"That was great!" said Tully. "Too bad he didn't come a few hours sooner, so I could have made my date with Wendy."

"Better than spending the night here." Samster paused. "Did that guy look familiar to you?"

"Actually, now that you mention it, he was kind of familiar, but I can't place him. How about you?"

"I think he was one of the people who lived out near Crazy Tony that we asked directions from."

Tully thought, then frowned. "I hope we didn't look familiar to him."

#

On their way back to Albuquerque, Tully turned to Samster. "I've come to a decision."

"Good, so have I." Tully raised his eyebrows. "You go first," Samster said.

Tully eyed Samster suspiciously, then said, "I'm going to come clean with Wendy. I'm not going to try to concoct an excuse. It probably wouldn't work anyway, but even if it did, I'm tired of feeling like a shit for deceiving her. If we're going to be married, she deserves a husband she can trust. Okay, now what's your decision?"

"Same thing. She deserves a friend she can trust."

Tully grinned. "That's great! Then we can confess together, it'll be safer that way."

"Sorry," said Samster. "This is one of those things you have to do by yourself."

#

Wendy didn't frown or glare at Tully when she opened the door to her apartment, her face a stolid mask. He looked past her to see if someone might be visiting, but he saw only her desk uncharacteristically cluttered with paper. She should have been claws-out furious, but she just looked at him. Tully was worried.

"Hi, Wendy," he said, assuming his most winsome smile. "I know I'm late, and I'm sorry, but I was with Samster in my mother's car when its battery died, and we had to wait a long time for someone with jumper cables."

Wendy looked skeptical. "And where did that happen?"

"That's something I need to tell you. Let's go sit down."

He followed her into the kitchen, where they both sat at the table. She didn't offer him tea or something to eat but simply waited. He thought he detected some redness around her eyes.

Tully laced his fingers together on the table top. "Well, yes, the battery in Mom's car, it did die, but there's more to it than just that. It happened down near Socorro. We'd driven down to look for the claim that Lester Toler had in the Chupadera Mountains, the claim we found looking in the Bureau of Geology library."

He paused, waiting for a reaction. There was none, so he pressed on.

"We weren't going to tell you, as we'd intended just a quick trip, but driving back I realized that I didn't want to deceive you, even with a lie of omission. Samster reached the same conclusion."

She just nodded. He saw her eyes begin to water.

"I'm sorry, Wendy, I really am. I know I said I wouldn't do anything more with the Lost Oro Mine, but we just had to follow that lead, and you know what, it panned out. We found something, a rock ..."

"I don't care," she interrupted. "I don't care what you found." Tears now were streaming down her cheeks. "I suspected you were off somewhere because I tried calling you and got no answer. And I'm glad you and Samster decided to be straight with me, but you can go off and do whatever you want with that stupid Lost Oro or whatever you want to call it. It doesn't matter anymore."

Tears now were flowing freely now, but her voice was steady. "I can't go on like this. Our relationship is going nowhere. Whenever I get hopeful, whenever I begin to think things will change, something happens to remind me that things aren't going to change—and I just can't take it any more." She sniffed and wiped her eyes with her sleeve.

"Today was a bad day, Tully, a *really* bad day. I needed you, and you were off treasure hunting with Samster. That's how it's been, and that's how it will always be."

"Wendy ..." Tully stammered.

"No, don't say anything, there's nothing to say. This has gone beyond apologies and promises and make-you-feel-better gestures. I've given this a lot of thought, and it hasn't been easy, but I feel clear about this. Tully, we need to move on with our lives—separately."

She paused and again wiped tears from her eyes. Tully sat stunned. He started to say something but before he could speak she said, "I still love you, Tully, and that's something I'll just have to deal with.

"But for now it's best if we don't see each other for a while. Later, we can talk, and probably should, but now is not the time, so I'd appreciate it if you'd leave. I'm not kicking you out, I've just got important things I've got to take care of, and I need to be alone."

She rose and returned to her desk in the living room. Tully showed himself out.

She went to her desk and started to pick up papers but instead dissolved into tears. Oh, God, it had been harder than she'd expected, but at least she hadn't lost it in front of him.

Now she had to pull it together again. The crisis at school wouldn't wait.

CHAPTER 17

Samster scowled as he steered his bicycle across campus, ignoring the Dismount signs. He locked his bike in a rack in front of the Norton Center for Earth and Planetary Sciences. From his backpack he took the rock sample from Black Canyon, looked at it, felt its heft. It was heavier than a normal rock, wasn't it?

He returned it to his backpack as he walked up the building's front steps. Once he'd fixed the bike of a geology grad student, Brad, and now he was calling in the favor.

It was still early in the morning, but Samster's curiosity about the rock overcame his normal habits, and he knew he was more likely to catch Brad alone now, and indeed Brad was by himself in the geology lab. He motioned Samster in.

Rocks of all sizes and shapes littered the room—on the floor, on tables, in boxes. Most were dull brown or gray. Brad was attaching labels to samples in a tray.

"Hey, Sam the Man"—Samster loathed that nickname but had ceased fighting it—"look at this." He held out to Samster a dusty brown rock the approximate shape of a saucer.

"It's awesome, Brad, what is it?"

Brad chuckled. "You probably didn't notice, but that sample's just loaded with graptolites, *Stolonoidea* to be exact."

"Well, why didn't you just say so, I'd recognize them anywhere."

"Okay, okay, I guess you have to be a geologist to get excited about things like graptolites, but here, look." Using a small brush he dusted the rock's surface to reveal what resembled numerous sections of pencil lead. "Those babies were alive in the middle-Cambrian, over half a billion years ago."

"Holding up pretty well, considering," said Samster.

Brad laughed. "You didn't come here just to be impressed by important evidence of the Cambrian explosion, when life on Earth really took off. Seriously, one of those little guys might be your ancestor, or mine."

"Probably yours, matches your eyes better."

"All right, what have you got for me?"

Samster dug into his backpack and withdrew the rock sample. He handed it to Brad.

"Dacite," said Brad. "Pretty common in volcanic areas such as the Rio Grande Valley."

"Look closer."

Brad took the sample over to a table where a large magnifying glass lay. "It appears to be mineralized, little flecks of something."

"Any idea what?"

"Hard to say without doing chemical analysis. Could be pyrite, or peridot crystals, or ..." He paused, looking closer. "Where'd you get this?"

"Guy at a craft fair gave it to my mother, she traded a coffee mug for it. He said it might be valuable. Yeah, sure, but I promised her I'd have someone look at it."

Brad hefted the rock in his palm. "Just a minute."

He took the rock to where a microscope sat on a table. "Mind if I scratch off just a tiny piece of this?"

Samster hesitated, then said, "Sure, go for it—but as little as you can."

With a pocketknife Brad scraped a few fragments onto a glass slide, which he then positioned under the microscope. He flicked a switch, illuminating the slide. He peered through the eyepiece.

A long silence as he moved the rock beneath the lens. Then, "Where'd you say you got this?"

"Guy at a craft fair gave it to my mom in payment for a cup."

"Must've been quite a cup."

"What do you mean?"

Unless I'm mistaken the little flecks in here are gold."

Samster's mouth dropped.

"Yeah, it's pretty rare when you can actually see the gold in a piece of ore. My guess is that you've got a piece of high grade."

Seeing Samster's puzzlement Brad continued. "Gold miners measure ore in ounces of gold per ton of rock, usually invisible before smelting, but sometimes you get veins where the minerals are concentrated. Miners will pick out samples from there.

"Of course, those rocks aren't representative of the whole mine, that's why they're called high-grade, but because the samples sometimes are spectacular they're worth more than the minerals in them. They keep them or sell them to rock shops. Too bad your mom doesn't know where this came from, she definitely should hang onto it."

He handed the sample back to Samster, who took it as if it were radioactive.

"Yeah," Brad said as Samster shuffled to the door, as if in a daze, "if your mom sees that guy again, she should ask him where that came from. And if he knows, then come tell me. A few of those rocks would pay for a new bike."

#

Tully sat straight and upright in a wooden chair in his apartment. It was an uncomfortable chair that everyone avoided, but today he felt drawn to it, as if he deserved its discomfort. He briefly shook his head, then resumed staring at nothing. He hadn't moved for an hour.

He only looked up when a knock sounded at the door and he heard Samster's voice, "Open up, dude."

Without waiting Samster pushed open the door and barged in, his face beaming. "Listen, man, have I got something ..." He stopped abruptly. "What's wrong?"

"Wendy broke up with me."

"Oh, no. That can't be."

"It is."

"What happened?"

Tully told him.

"I can't comprehend this. You and Wendy ... you're like the Earth and the Moon."

Tully didn't see any humor in the comparison. He wasn't sure he'd see humor in anything again.

"I deserved it." He started to cry, then caught himself. "I've been late before, but something bad happened to her yesterday, and I wasn't there for her. I was off with you looking for gawdammed rocks." He slammed his fist into his palm. "I've taken her for granted, assumed she'd always give me another chance if I looked sorry enough, gave her gifts, made her laugh. And promises, she always bought my worthless promises."

He paused to collect himself. "Now I don't have anything."

"Did she say what bad thing happened to her?"

Tully shook his head. "She didn't want to. Probably didn't see any point. I wasn't there when it mattered. Now that we're finished, there's no reason to tell me. I'm worried sick about her. Whatever it is, it's serious—and she shouldn't have to face it alone.

"Samster, she asked me to leave, said she wasn't kicking me out but had something important to deal with."

Samster reached for Tully's hand. "No. I won't accept that you two are finished. Maybe I can talk to her. After all, I was as guilty as you."

"Please don't. Not on my account. You're not as guilty as I am. I screwed up, and now it's something only I can deal with, even if I don't know how."

Then to change the subject Tully said, "You said you had something for me?"

Samster looked bleak. "I do have something, but now is not the time." He went over and gave his friend a quick shoulder hug. "Don't give up. And don't do anything rash." And with that he quickly left the apartment.

#

Samster noticed Wendy's car in her driveway as he pedaled past her house from Tully's apartment. School would have started two hours ago; she shouldn't be home. He told himself he hadn't intended to go this route, but he knew better.

He didn't know what he should do. Tully probably was right when he'd urged Samster not to say anything to Wendy on his behalf—but he still was a friend to both of them. Besides, Tully had mentioned that something bad had happened to Wendy. As her friend he had to learn what.

Wendy opened the door at his knock. She looked terrible, her eyes puffy and red, her mouth tight and grim. He'd never seen her like this before.

"Hi, no school today?" He couldn't bring himself to remark how bad she looked.

"Oh, there's school, just not for me. I'm afraid I can't invite you in right now, I have things I have to get done as soon as possible."

"I just came from Tully's."

She stood silently, then said, "Okay, come on in, but I do have urgent work to do." When Samster was seated on the couch she looked directly at him. "How's he taking it?"

"Oh, it's nothing that suicide wouldn't cure. Come on, Wendy, how do you think he's taking it? You're everything to him. Sure, he's clumsy and obtuse and sometimes insensitive, though not deliberately. And he's sure done a lot of stupid things lately—so have I—and I don't blame you for being pissed at him. But breaking up with him, leaving him ..."

"I just couldn't take it anymore. If I'm everything to him, as you say, why'd he go prospecting? I needed him, dammit, and he was off looking at rocks."

"He didn't know you needed him, he'd have been here if he had."

"But sometimes you can't know when you're going to need someone, you just have to trust that they'll be there.

I tried calling him all afternoon yesterday, even after I realized he wasn't around. That's been the story of my life with him—and I've had it. He apologizes and promises to be better and buys me flowers or silly cards, which I love— but he never changes. It's time for me to move on. I've got very difficult stuff to deal with right now."

"Such as?"

"It's nothing you, or Tully, need to be concerned about, especially not Tully."

"Come on, Wendy, I care about you—Tully cares about you—and he's right: whatever this is you shouldn't have to face it alone. Now let's have it."

Her eyes looked at the floor, then up. "You remember I told you once about Brendan, the class bully?"

Tully nodded. "The kid who gets off on making other kids cry and then laughing at them? Sadistic little brat."

"That's him. He usually stops short of physical torment, at least when the teachers are around. We've talked to his parents, couple of high-end personal injury lawyers—you've seen their faces on highway billboards— but they just shrug it off, saying it's just kidding, horse play. He's their 'precious,' when they can spare time for him, that is.

"Well, yesterday he crossed the line. He chose Eli for his victim, sweet little kid but small, a year younger than Brendan. He stutters occasionally, and Brendan was mocking his speaking. I was in the room and warned Brendan to lay off, but when I turned my back he persisted until finally poor Eli snapped. I turned around to see him lunge at Brendan. He missed, fell on the floor, and then Brendan leaped on him, straddled him, began hitting him.

"I screamed, grabbed Brendan, and dragged him off. I was furious. Poor Eli was crying—and that sadistic little bastard Brendan was laughing. As I dragged Brendan off he lost his balance, went down, and hit his head on a desk corner. A cut above his eye. It started bleeding.

"That was when Sally, the teacher in the next room, came in. I'd picked Brendan up to see if he was okay, but he was flailing and screaming that I'd hit him. Another teacher arrived, and the three of us finally subdued Brendan. Sally had to force him into a chair and hold him there.

"I moved to comfort Eli, who'd been forgotten. He continued sobbing. By this time, the whole school knew something was up, and the principal came in. We all agreed we needed to call Eli's and Brendan's parents."

Wendy paused. Her fists were clenched, her lips a thin, tight line. Samster reached over and touched her arm. She looked up, forced a smile. "I'm okay." Then she shook her head, "What am I saying, I'm *not* okay, not even close.

"Before the parents arrived I tried to explain to Betty, the principal, what had happened. She and everyone else knew Brendan and despised him, but there he was, sitting there crying, blood seeping through the bandage we'd put on his cut, which I must say was minor.

"Eli's mom, she's a single parent, arrived first. She was good with Eli, comforted him, but she was furious with the school, said she'd spoken before about her son being bullied and teased. She was right. She had voiced complaints.

"But her anger was *nothing* compared to Brendan's parents. They demanded to know why an ambulance hadn't been called. And then, being tort lawyers, they threatened lawsuits. Against the school—and against me. Needless to say, I couldn't continue teaching there, I'm on leave of absence, paid for now, but that isn't likely to last.

"So now I'm looking for a legal defense. That, and wondering how I can go on with my life after I lost both my job and my fiancé on the same day."

And with that she dissolved into sobs.

CHAPTER 18

As Wendy walked toward her car across the parking lot of the law offices of Attorney Estella Mondragon and Associates, she noticed a dead bird on the pavement, one wing pointed upward as if in defiance of its fate. That's me, she thought.

Attorney Mondragon had just told her that while Brendan's cut was minor, the Bendermans certainly would produce photos of blood-soaked bandages, and in the eyes of the law, her defense of poor little Eli against a sadistic bully was irrelevant.

"Eli was the first one to make physical contact," Attorney Mondragon said, "and you initiated physical contact with Brendan. That his hitting his head was an accident doesn't mitigate your responsibility, at least in the eyes of the law."

Wendy'd sagged. "So I'm doomed."

"It doesn't look good. The most encouraging thing I can say is that you're fortunate in not having any assets. That means the Bendermans' main target will be the school. Their pockets are much deeper than yours."

Wendy just stared at the dead bird. It just got worse. Not only was she going to be destitute but also she would be responsible for the financial catastrophe that would befall the school. They would try to cover their asses by terminating her—and she couldn't blame them. No one else would hire her. Her career was over almost before it had begun.

Before entering her car she carefully picked up the dead bird and placed it beneath a flowering bush.

#

After meeting with the lawyer, Wendy could not go home but went instead to a coffee shop. Her favorite coffee shop was a funky place called Jittery Joe's, but it was where she and Tully went, and she was afraid she might encounter him there. Instead she went to a Starbuck's on the first level of an upscale galleria near the law offices.

As she sat in an overstuffed chair and sipped her Zen green tea, hoping it might bring needed serenity and clarity, she looked at the baristas behind the counter. They probably made not much less money than she did as a pre-school teacher, with comparable benefits, but without the tantrums and soiled pants and bathroom pissing contests. Could she be a barista?

And could this be the first sign of acceptance that what had happened wasn't just a bump in her life but the terminal car wreck of her career?

She'd expected to be devastated by the realization, but curiously she was exhilarated. She recalled a line from a song: "Freedom's just another word for nothing left to lose."

She'd never actually chosen pre-school education as a career but had merely acquiesced in her parents' urgings that it would be a good, pragmatic choice. She liked little kids, or at least thought she did, but her passion had been photography, and she'd even taken an introductory class at the university. Pre-school education, however, was much more practical. And given Tully, practicality certainly had strong appeal.

Now it didn't matter what her parents thought, or whether she needed to anchor Tully. Finally she was free— because she had nothing left to lose.

#

As Samster steered his bicycle into his home's driveway he saw that Elron's bicycle was there as well, a good sign as the family had talked about getting window repairs done on the room that had been Richard's, and Elron was to be at home when the workmen arrived. But though Elron was there, the workmen apparently weren't; no truck was in the driveway.

"Hey, little bro," said Samster as he breezed into the kitchen where Elron sat at the table in front of a laptop computer, "where are the workmen? Don't tell me they've finished already."

"We wish," muttered his brother, not looking up. Samster waited him out. Finally Elron said, "They came back with the estimate Mom had requested, and it was more money than we have right now, so Mom canceled the order."

"Shit!" Samster slammed his fist on the kitchen counter. "If we don't get that place fixed up and rented we're screwed.

Elron just looked at him bleakly. "Maybe we can rent it to a handyman."

"We did that once, remember? That was supposed to be part of the deal with Richard, that he'd help with maintenance—and look how that turned out. We're just lucky his 'bad back'"—he made air quotes with his fingers— "prevented him from doing more maintenance."

Samster paced around the kitchen while Elron resumed tinkering with the laptop. Finally he said, "I'm going to Wobbling Wally's to see if I can get more work."

As he was going out the door Elron said, "Oh, I forgot to tell you a man came by this afternoon looking for you."

Samster stopped, turned around. He couldn't think of any man who he would want looking for him except Tully— and Elron knew Tully.

"Did he leave a message?"

"Nah. Said he'd catch you later."

"Well, then, describe him, dammit."

Elron described Crazy Tony. "I didn't like him. He stank."

"Shit!" said Samster as he left.

CHAPTER 19

Samster was truing a bicycle wheel when the door to Wobbling Wally's opened and Crazy Tony entered. His eyes found Samster, who nodded and tried to return to work.

"Hi there, little feller," Tony said in a deep gravelly voice. His smile revealed a gap in his upper front teeth. The other people in the bike shop paused to stare at him; clearly he hadn't come to look at expensive Italian road bikes.

Samster muttered hi, tried to return to work. Tony clomped in his dirty work boots to where Samster stood.

"Aw, come on, little feller, I know you remember me. You was awfully talkative at my place." He leered at Samster. "I stopped by here the other day to tell you I had information about that dacite you was interested in. I know you didn't find any dacite in the Chupadera Mountains after seeing me—my friend Carl told me he'd helped you out of a bad spot when your car battery went dead. I know mountains where there's a lot of dacite. Could be profitable poking around there."

Samster stopped working and motioned Tony aside. The others in the bike shop pretended to resume work. "No, we didn't find any dacite. It was just a lark, an excuse to get out and go hiking."

"You don't need to go all the way to the Chupaderas to go hiking," Tony leered. "Or go to the geology library."

Samster cringed. He'd been caught. "My friend Tully is a historian, he's interested in old mines, he thought we might locate some in the Chupaderas, but it was a waste of time, we found nothing."

"But you did find something. When I was by here the other day the guys here told me you was showing them a rock, a real pretty rock with metal flecks in it."

Samster felt his face go flush. "Oh, that. That was just a mineralized rock we found in one of the prospect holes. Had pyrite in it. I keep things like that around the house."

"I'd like to see that rock," Tony said.

"Bummer," said Samster. "Tully teased me about the metal flakes being just pyrite so I tossed it."

"Where'd you toss it?"

"Oh, just a dumpster, somewhere," Samster stammered.

Tony's eyes narrowed. "Why don't you go look for it? It takes the trained eye of an experienced prospector to know what's really in a rock. I might even buy it from you. I'm always interested in samples of ...'pyrite'."

"Uh, I'll try ... but they might have emptied the dumpster by now. I wouldn't wait up over it."

"Oh, but I will. I'm *really* interested in that sample. I'll swing by your house again to see if you found it. Maybe your mother or brother will know where you tossed it. I'll ask them, if you're not there." There was no mistaking the implied threat in his voice.

Turning abruptly Tony left the bicycle shop.

Rusty, one of Wally's other mechanics, put his tools down and said to Samster, "That was one rough-looking dude. I hope you can find that sample for him. I wouldn't want him coming after my family." He paused. "And he stank."

Samster just stared at the door.

#

Tully sat at his rickety wooden table and stared at Samster. "Let me get this straight. That rock we found really does have gold in it, you told your bike-shop buddies about it ..."

"I didn't tell them about the gold," Samster interrupted, "I just showed them the rock and pointed out the metal flecks, I didn't tell them I'd confirmed they were gold."

"... and now Crazy Tony knows about the rock, has come looking for you and threatened your family? Now he'll keep looking for you, and probably me? Hell, he might even come after Wendy, since he knows she's my girlfriend—or was."

Samster stared at the floor, his normal wacky exuberance absent. Tully had never seen him so deflated. Then his eyes rose to meet Tully's.

"That's the other thing I need to tell you. I went to see Wendy and got her to tell me what happened. It's bad, man, really bad. Dealing with Crazy Tony is the last thing she needs right now."

"Tell me, Samster, I need to know."

"You do need to know," said Samster, "but Wendy should be the one to tell you. She'll probably resist talking to you, but she really needs you. Even if you can't get back together, she still needs you—and you need to warn her about Crazy Tony."

#

Tully didn't expect to find Wendy at home when he went to her house, but her car was in the driveway, and she opened the door when he knocked. Her eyes were red, but otherwise her face was blank. Tully wanted to cry when he saw her.

"Wendy, I know you don't want to see me, and I don't blame you, but we need to talk. May I come in?"

She held the door open for him. "It's not that I don't want to see you, it's just that I don't think it's a good idea right now."

"Probably not," Tully said as he entered and stood before her, "but I just talked to Samster, and he told me that you're facing something really serious, and even if we're not a couple anymore, you need to have someone beside you as you go into it. That means me, and Samster."

She sat on the couch, and motioned for Tully to sit beside her. "Yeah, it's pretty bad, but ..."

"But nothing," Tully said, "I let you down once, I won't do it again. Samster and I are here for you, whether you like it or not. He'd be here now, except that I wanted to see you alone first. He wouldn't tell me what happened, said it would be better if I heard it from you. And there's something else we need to deal with together."

Wendy started to cry. "Oh, Tully, I've missed you, but I'm so confused." And then in a spate of tears she related what had happened with Brandon and Eli at the school and what her lawyer had said.

"Whoa! That *is* bad. But we'll take it one day at a time. What does your lawyer recommend?"

"I've done most of what she said—contacting other teachers who have witnessed Brendan's bullying, though most of them aren't eager to get involved. We're in touch

176

with Eli's parents and their lawyer. They're more cooperative. They're not enthusiastic about helping out the school, since they have their own lawsuit against it, but they're at least willing to cooperate with me. After all, it was while I was defending Eli that this all happened.

"It will take a while for depositions to be taken and motions to be made. My lawyer told me not to do anything in the meantime. But doing nothing is really hard. Now, what was that other thing you wanted to tell me about?"

Tully grimaced. "I'm afraid it grew out of that misguided trip to Socorro. It has to do with that rock we found at Lester Toler's claim. It turns out to have gold in it. A lot, for the size of the rock. Samster took it to a geologist friend, and they actually could see flecks of gold."

Wendy's eyes widened. "That's *terrible!*"

"Terrible? That rock has real gold in it! If we can find where it came from, our problems are solved."

Rage replaced surprise on Wendy's face. "Oh, so that gold is going to write your dissertation for you? So now you're going to toss everything into the wind and go looking for this lost gold mine as the solution to all your problems? And I'm supposed to see this as good news?"

"But, but ..." He hung his head. "You're right. I'm doing it again. But surely you can see that this rock demands to be investigated. I guarantee Samster won't forget about it. Has he told you about his family's financial predicament? Finding gold really would solve his problems."

"Then let him look for it."

"Wendy, you know I can't do that, any more than I can let you face this school problem by yourself."

Wendy shook her head, wiped the hair out of her eyes. "Then I don't want any part of this—including you. I told you once I'm done with the distractions, the promises, the false hopes of you getting serious. I don't have time in my life for another wild-goose gold chase."

Tully put his hand on hers. "Wendy, you can't know how much I don't want to tell you this, but I'm afraid it's not that simple." He told her about Crazy Tony and Samster.

"He'll come looking for me—and will find me. And it's possible he'll come for you too, since he knows you're my girlfriend—or were."

"Crazy Tony! Just what I need!" She put her hands to her forehead. "Just what I need." Then she unfastened the pendant around her neck in which she'd had mounted the piece of gold Tully had given her on the Rio Grande. She unfastened it and tossed it at him.

"Here, I don't want this. It's just a reminder of this whole gold-seeking sickness and how this mess with Tony started."

Tully held the pendant, then muttered, "I'm sorry to say your instincts regarding him were correct. We should have stayed away from him."

"I'm going to spend a lot more time listening to *my* instincts. Now, again, as I told you, I have important things to do." She stood and turned away.

Tully held the pendant, his eyes watering, then he turned toward the door. At the last minute he said, "At least promise me you'll be careful. I don't know where Tony is or what his plans are, but he's unpredictable and dangerous."

When Tully walked down the driveway he didn't notice a beat-up pickup pulling away from around the corner.

#

After Tully left, Wendy had a good cry, then she dried her eyes and tried to think through what she needed to do. She realized she didn't have the luxury of doing nothing. Tully and Samster might be in danger, and though they'd brought this on themselves, through their own colossal stupidity, she still loved both of them.

She felt her neck, where the pendant had hung. She wished she hadn't been so impulsive in giving it back to him, though perhaps it was necessary to convey to him how she really had had enough.

But the pendant and resolving issues with Tully could wait. Now she had to deal with Crazy Tony.

CHAPTER 20

Tully waited until the second ring before he picked up the phone, a habit he'd heard called *telecrastination.*

"Tully, we've got to do something about Tony," Wendy said. "I know I told you yesterday I didn't want any part of this, but for better or worse we're all in this together."

"I'm afraid you're right. I've never seen Samster like this, he's just overwhelmed with worry—and fear. I wish Tony had just come for me, I'm the one responsible for all this."

"Yes, you are," said Wendy but without bitterness. "And the mess I'm in with the school is wholly mine, and Samster has his own issues with his family. But as I said, we're all in everything together, so let's forget about who's responsible for what and get on with dealing with it. Unfortunately, I don't have any ideas."

"I might have one."

"Yes?" said Wendy with audible skepticism.

Tully continued. "Tony is focused on that stupid rock, and he's pretty sure Samster didn't throw it in a dumpster, like he claimed. So we have to get another rock, a worthless one, that will back up Samster's story that the rock we found really is just filled with pyrite, not gold. We can't just go to a rock shop and buy a pyrite sample. Tony knows we were looking in the Chupaderas, and he'll spot anything that doesn't match their geology."

"I think I see where this is heading. We've got to go back to the Chupaderas and bring back another rock."

"Right," said Tully, "but it can't be just any rock. It's got to have pyrite in it, and I'm not sure we can find one."

"And if we can't find one?"

"Then we'll go to a rock shop in Socorro and see what we can get."

Wendy hesitated before speaking. "I don't like it. My instincts are saying this is just going deeper into a hole that's already too deep."

"Any other ideas?" Her silence was her answer.

Tully continued. "And when you say 'us'?"

"I mean the three of us. I'm not letting you two out of my sight."

#

Wendy was underwhelmed by Lester Toler's prospect hole. "*This* is where you were when I was losing my career and needed you?"

Tully shriveled.

"It doesn't look like much," said Samster, "but don't forget that a rock we found here did have gold in it—even if the rock didn't come from here."

Wendy just scowled. "Now let's see if we can find a rock that has fool's gold in it."

After an hour of examining rocks not only in that hole but others along the ridge leading to it, Tully sat on a boulder in exasperation. "For a mineral that's supposed to be common, pyrite is conspicuously absent here."

After another hour of examining rocks they gave up. "Looks like we have to resort to Plan B."

"Which is?" asked Wendy.

"We go to a local rock shop and buy a rock from the Chupaderas that has pyrite in it."

"I still don't like it," said Wendy. "We're too visible, and there's a good chance Tony will hear about it."

"I don't like it either," said Tully, "but if we don't show Tony something he'll keep badgering us. He knows we found something, and he doesn't buy Samster's dumpster story."

Wendy frowned, then shrugged. "Let's go—but I have this horrible feeling that by trying to get out of this hole we're just digging ourselves deeper."

#

Two hours later Tully emerged from a scruffy "Rock Shop" at the edge of Socorro carrying a dark baseball-sized rock that the shop's owner, as scruffy as the shop itself, had said definitely was from the Chupaderas. "Look at that," Tully said to Wendy and Samster, "the pyrite is pretty visible in there. I had to do fast talking explaining why I wanted an essentially worthless rock from the Chupaderas, but I told him I was teaching a local high school geology class.

Samster was exuberant, Wendy less so. "I'll show this to the guys at Wobblin' Wally's and ask them forget about the other rock."

As Wendy began driving toward the highway leading north to Albuquerque, Tully said, "We have one more thing to do before leaving Socorro. We should go to the local newspaper to search its files."

"What?" exclaimed Wendy.

"We need to find out more about Tony. I know you think this is getting in deeper with him, but he already knows a lot about us. The more we know about him, the better prepared we'll be. I think we're being naive if we think just showing him a rock will satisfy him."

Wendy's mind reeled. This was not going as she'd planned. Reluctantly she asked Samster. "It's your call, since you're the one who'll show him the rock you supposedly retrieved from the dumpster."

"I think Tully's right. He'll still be suspicious when I show him the rock. Right now we don't know much about him. As Sir Francis Bacon said, knowledge is power."

Not for the first time Wendy wondered where a slacker like Samster came up with things like that. But he had a point. "Okay, let's go, but we don't even know his last name. We can't go to the newspaper and ask to do a search on 'Crazy Tony'."

Tully laughed. "Actually, I wouldn't be surprised if the newspaper knows exactly who we're talking about."

#

The Socorro *Sentinel* was located in a one-story modern brick building two blocks east of Main Street. It had the charm of a laundromat, but the receptionist was friendly.

"Yes, we had all the back issues digitized two years ago, so you should be able to find anyone mentioned in the paper. There's a terminal in the newsroom. There's no charge for a search, but we do charge if you want to print the results."

"We have a bit of a problem," said Tully. "We know the first name of the man we're searching for, but not his last name, though we think he's been around Socorro for a while. He's a miner and prospector, lives near the southern edge of town, not the friendliest character, kind of an outlaw type actually." Tully was tempted to make up a story about how they were doing genealogical research but for once decided not to stray from the truth. "His first name's Tony."

The woman behind the counter frowned, eyed the three suspiciously, then relaxed somewhat when her eyes fell on Wendy. "I think you mean Tony Kalvari."

"Big guy, doesn't shave much, kind of scruffy ... stinks ... and like I said, not exactly a Welcome Wagon sort of guy."

"That fits. Let's go see what we've got."

She led to a large open area in which were about a dozen desks, each with a computer terminal on it. At several were men and women typing. Near the back was a desk also with a computer terminal. She sat, typed commands, then said, "There, now you're in the archives. Do you know how to use something like this?"

"I do," said Tully.

"Then go to it," the woman said as she pulled up chairs for Wendy and Samster.

The search for Kalvari returned several hits, most from municipal court: public intoxication, DWI, assault, assault with a deadly weapon, threatening. He'd spent time in the county jail.

"Whoa! Not exactly your citizen-of-the-year type," exclaimed Samster.

Wendy was simply aghast.

They were interrupted by a middle-aged man who'd been sitting at a keyboard when they'd entered room. "I couldn't help overhearing your interest in Tony Kalvari. I'm acquainted with him—because I cover the courts for the paper. I hope your interest isn't genealogical, because he's definitely not someone you want near the trunk of your family tree."

"Oh, no," said Tully. "It's a very remote connection, like in the Pleistocene."

The reporter chuckled, then frowned. "I'm kind of a rockhound, and when I moved to Socorro I made the mistake of linking up with Tony to go rockhounding. We went into the Magdalena Mountains and found interesting specimens. Tony managed to make off with all of them. When I went to get them at his place, he sicced his dogs on me. Stay away from him."

Samster spoke, "Believe me, that's exactly what we plan to do." The reporter eyed Samster.

Tully changed the subject. "I can see the court record certainly backs you up. That's quite a rap sheet."

The reporter looked at Tully. "Those are just the incidents that made it to court. But the judges are finally beginning to take issue with him being a public menace. If you look closely at the last entry you'll notice the judge put him on strict probation after sending him to the lockup for two months, told him he'd go to prison if he violated the probation conditions. And I know this judge, he'll do it. Tony will have a Santa Fe zip code if he messes up again."

Wendy spoke. "Trust us, we want to keep as far away as possible from him."

"We call him Crazy Tony," offered Samster.

The reporter again eyed Samster with curiosity as he walked back to his desk.

"Well, that pretty much confirms our worst suspicions about Tony," said Wendy. "Let's get back to Albuquerque and discuss what we're going to do."

"Wait," said Tully, "as long as we're here we should search for Lester Toler, try to learn about him."

Wendy radiated exasperation. "Give it up! Look at the mess we're in already because of this crazy gold mine quest."

Tully's eyes appealed to Samster. "Well, we are here ..."

Tully's fingers already were typing. "Look, they have two entries. One is from November 18, 1880." They crowded around the screen, even Wendy.

"The sheriff's office is continuing to investigate the disappearance of a local resident. Lester Toler, who lives alone in a shack on the southern outskirts of Socorro, was discovered missing when neighbors complained about dogs barking. Upon investigation they found Toler's three dogs in bad condition, having been without food or water for several days.

"Toler, a prospector and employee of several mines in New Mexico, has been in the Socorro area for several years and has been known to leave on prospecting trips, usually in the eastern part of the county, but never for this long and never without providing for his dogs if he doesn't take them. He is known to have had a mule, also missing.

"The sheriff's office is not saying foul play is suspected. Toler is described as of medium build, about 60 years of age, with a long gray beard, and a characteristic limp.

They are asking residents with information about Toler's whereabouts to come forward."

Then three months later another brief story:

"The sheriff's office has said no leads have been received regarding the disappearance three months ago of Lester Toler. They have contacted the mines where he is known to have worked, but none has reported seeing him. The investigation is ongoing."

"Whoa!" said Samster. "We should go to his shack."

"No!" barked Wendy. Tully and Samster gaped at her. "We're going back to Albuquerque. We've done what we came to do."

As they started to leave the newsroom, Tully said, "Just a minute." He walked to the reporter's desk. "If you're a rockhound, maybe you can help us with something. We're rockhounds too, interested in the geology of this area. Do you know any mountains in the area that have dacite?"

Wendy glowered at him. Samster hovered.

"I've heard dacite is a good rock for mineral specimens," Tully continued.

The reporter looked skeptically at Tully. Finally he said, "I don't know who told you that, dacite usually is pretty barren, but yeah, there are mountains here that have dacite. The Magdalenas have dacite, so do the Bear Mountains. To the east there's dacite in the Sierra Oscura—and the Sierra del Sombre are almost all dacite.

"But like I said, most rockhounds consider dacite pretty monotonous stuff." He paused. "Maybe you know something we don't."

"No," said Tully. "We're amateurs, I mean *real* amateurs. We'll find other places to look. Thanks for all your help." He and Samster and Wendy started to walk away.

"Don't you want suggestions?" he called after them. Then in a louder voice he cried, "Stay away from Tony Kalvari."

#

Wendy drove in sullen silence after leaving Socorro. Tully tried to ease the tension. "I understand why you're upset—and I don't blame you ..."

With vehemence that shocked both Tully and Samster she said, "Oh, just *stop* it. I'm just sick of it. Every time you do something that you know makes me upset you say, 'I don't blame you.' That's just an immature, cowardly way of avoiding responsibility. And in the past it's always worked. It kind of pulls the plug on my anger. But it never stops you from doing it again."

Tully could only stammer. "But I was only trying to show understanding of how you feel."

"If you really understood how I feel—or cared—you wouldn't do these things. I was appalled at what you pulled in the newspaper. 'We're rockhounds too.' And looking up that old miner. Yeah, Lester Toler's disappearance is kind of a mystery, but so what? It's over 100 years old. They couldn't solve it then."

Samster said, "But it was kind of interesting. This guy scribbles a map to a gold mine, and then he disappears."

"I repeat: So what?" Looking directly Tully she said, "Is Lester Toler going to write your dissertation?

"And *then* you have to go ask that reporter about what mountains have dacite. So what are you going to do now? Drop out of school so you can go wandering around the ranges looking at all the dacite outcrops?"

"But we have a map," Tully said.

"You don't even know which mountains it's to. And stop saying 'we'. I'm not in this treasure hunt anymore, if I ever was. I'm here only because of needing to do something about Crazy Tony."

Tully was shocked into silence. Samster, trying to defuse Wendy's anger said, "At least we found about Tony, Tony Kalvari that is."

Wendy turned on him. "Yeah, we know that he's every bit as scary and dangerous as we thought he was."

"Yes, but we also know that if he pulls something we can send him to prison."

"For some reason I don't find that very reassuring," said Wendy.

Finally Tully spoke. "Wendy's right. Prisons are filled with violent types who weren't deterred by the threat of a sentence. If they were rational, they wouldn't be there."

Samster said nothing. He gazed eastward, toward the distant mountain ranges. Under his breath he said, "I wonder if those are the Oscura Mountains, or the Sierra del Sombre."

CHAPTER 21

When Samster approached Wobblin' Wally's on his bicycle he saw Tony standing outside. He wished he could slide on this, but Tony saw him before he could turn.

"Just the feller I've been looking for," Tony said with faux friendliness. "Those fellers in there said you found that rock you tossed in the dumpster."

"I did, though I hope you appreciate me getting it for you, rummaging around in a dumpster is no fun—and besides the rock is worthless. The yellow metal in it is just pyrite. Fool's gold."

"I know what pyrite is. Let's see it."

Samster dug in his backpack, taking care not to disturb the real rock, which he'd placed in a so-called secret compartment. He handed the rock to Tony, who snatched it eagerly.

Tony peered at the rock, then at Samster.

"Yep, that's pyrite. Where'd you say you found this?"

"On a ridge, along Black Canyon."

"Mighty interesting. Mighty interesting. I've prospected all along that ridge, and I've never seen any rock like this there. In fact, the only place I've seen rock like this, with pyrite in it, is the Four Aces Mine, in the southern Chupaderas."

He paused, then peered sinisterly at Samster, "In fact, I might have seen this very rock before, because I sold a bunch of rocks from that mine to Harold Watson at the rock shop in Socorro."

Samster's mind froze. He opened his mouth but no words came out. Finally he stammered, "I don't know how that rock got on the ridge. There weren't any others like it there. That's why we picked it up. I didn't know it came from a mine."

"You're sure there's nothing you want to tell me about this rock you supposedly found? Maybe there's another rock you found?"

"Uh, no, not a thing."

Tony handed the rock back to Samster, then started to turn away. "I think I'll go have a chat with Harold. I sure hope you're telling the truth, because I don't take kindly to people I think are conning me."

As soon as Tony was out of sight Samster pulled out his cell phone and called Tully and Wendy. To both the message was the same: "We have to talk. Plan B backfired."

#

Tully turned his cell phone off as he entered Elnora's office. He knew that nothing irritated her more than a cell phone going off while she was talking face-to-face with someone.

She looked up from the papers she'd been reading when Tully entered. She looked worn, haggard, her mouth was grim. "Hello, Tully," she said. "Thanks for coming by on such short notice." She'd called him that morning and requested a meeting. "Please sit down."

With no preliminary chit-chat Elnora began. "Spencer's out to get you. Apparently the story of you calling him an asshole has spread throughout the college, and he imagines people laughing at him behind his back—which, in fact, they are.

"He sees the dissertation deadline as his means of getting back at you, as he's confident you have no hope of making it—given your record."

Tully winced.

"He's asking dissertation supervisors, meaning me specifically, to file progress reports, so I'm asking you: What progress have you made lately?"

"Uh ... things have been complicated lately ... " but Elnora interrupted him.

"So in other words you've made no progress, am I correct?"

Tully could only lower his head.

"You just don't get it, do you, Tully? You're a whisker away from throwing your entire academic career in the dumpster, and I can't save you. To be honest, I'm not sure I even want to. If you don't make deadline and are dropped from the program it will reflect badly on me and jeopardize my own standing in the department. Spencer would just *love* that."

"What do want me to do?" Tully whimpered.

"For starters, submit a detailed outline, along with a list of proposed references. Then get back down to Bean Country and gather original material. You'd said before that Wendy was going to take photos. That's the kind of thing that would impress the committee, if not Spencer.

"But above all else—*do it*! And if there's a word in there about some silly bean treasure, I personally will sign your dismissal papers."

#

Tully could barely stand as he made his way down the stairs from Elnora's office. He'd never before been presented with such an ultimatum. Always he'd been able to charm and talk his way into getting extensions, but he knew Elnora well enough to know that no longer was an option. What's more, he didn't want it to be. With Wendy dumping him, for the same reasons, he wanted to change, he *had* to change.

And he realized the person he most needed to stop gaming was himself.

#

"So Tony soon will find out that the rock we supposedly found in the Chupaderas actually came from the rock shop." The gaze Wendy leveled at Samster and Tully was pitiless. The two just stared bleakly at the floor of Tully's apartment.

She pushed her assault. "Crazy Tony, the guy who's armed, dangerous, vindictive, and unhinged. So now what? What's Plan C?"

Tully and Samster said nothing.

"How about this," Wendy said, "how about you come clean with him, give him the damned rock, tell him you found it at this Lester Toler character's prospect hole, and tell him he's welcome to do what he wants with it?"

Tully continued staring at the floor, but Samster raised his eyes and stared at Wendy. "But that rock has actual gold in it—and we found it. It's ours."

Wendy saw panic in Samster's eyes. She knew that against all common sense he was counting on the gold mine to solve his family's financial problems.

"How much gold? A couple of dollars worth? Wouldn't you pay that to get your life back?"

Samster stared at her with desperation, and Wendy realized Samster didn't have much of a life to get back, and that the gold represented the possibility of a new life.

"Besides," she added, "we don't know where that rock came from."

Finally Tully raised his head. "Actually, we do. It came from the place shown on the map."

Wendy rolled her eyes. "Oh, the map. I forgot about the map, the one showing mountains we don't even know the location of. How about this: you give him the map too. Then you're completely done."

"No!" said Tully and Samster together.

"We're *not* giving him the map," declared Samster.

Tully nodded. "That would be just giving in to thuggery, and that would be wrong. The map and the rock are rightfully ours—despite the stupid mistakes I've made."

"So what do you propose?" asked Wendy.

"I don't know," muttered Tully. "Maybe ... how about this, we get a restraining order against Tony, tell the judge he's been following and threatening us. Given Tony's history the courts in Socorro should be receptive."

"And how do you propose getting Tony into court?" countered Wendy. "And what do you say when he says he hasn't done anything, hasn't actually threatened us? And how do you think Tony will react to all this? And given his record, how compliant do you think he'll be with the court's orders?"

Tully said nothing. Finally he said, "I don't know what to do. But I'm afraid I can't deal with Tony right now." And he told them about Elnora's ultimatum.

"I've got to go to Bean Country, Tony or no Tony. Wendy, I'd like you to go with me, but that's up to you." He looked at Samster.

Then to his surprise Wendy said, "Actually, that's a great idea."

"It is?" said Samster.

"Sometimes when you don't know what to do the best thing is to do nothing," she said. "If we all got out of town for a few days it would give us time."

Samster appeared thoughtful, then said, "Getting out of town sounds like a good plan to me."

"Since my teaching career is crashing," said Wendy, "going back to Bean Country would allow me to do something I've been considering for a long time."

"And that is?" asked Tully.

"I never really wanted teaching as a career, I wanted to be a photographer. But Mom and Dad convinced me that teaching was much more practical. We can see how that turned out. Until now I didn't have the time or freedom to put together a portfolio, but I liked the photos I took on our trips there—"

"And Elnora thought your photos would be a very helpful addition to my dissertation, give the committee something concrete to look at."

"I'm happy to do that," Wendy continued, "but for once this is about me as much as it is about you. This can be a win-win for both of us. What about you, Samster?"

"I'd like to get out of town too," he said, "though my only role would be as go-fer. On the other hand, I'm good at that."

"No," said Tully. "You're more than that."

CHAPTER 22

"So this is Bean Country," said Samster from the back seat of Wendy's car. "It has all the mountain charm of the Chupaderas—without the mountains, or the charm."

"Don't be quick to judge," said Wendy. "It has its appeal."

"In a bean sort of way," said Tully.

"Real people lived real lives here," Wendy said. "It wouldn't hurt us to try to understand them better."

"I wasn't judging," grumped Samster. "You have to admit that it's good the people here had beans, because they weren't going to make it on eco-tourism.

"And I don't need to be reminded that the future is precarious," said Samster. "Just look at us. A month ago my family wasn't facing losing our home, Wendy wasn't losing her career, and Tully wasn't on the brink of being kicked out of school. Maybe we should buy a plot of land here and start homesteading."

Samster's comments put them into gray silence.

Tully brought them out of it by saying he needed a bladder break. "Willard is just a mile up the road," said Tully.

When they stopped in the parking area of a gas station that had been abandoned since gas was 69 cents a gallon, Wendy got out her photographic gear. "If I'm not mistaken, that's an old elevator for loading crops onto rail cars. Imagine the pride and excitement when that was just built. When was it built, Tully?"

"I don't know."

"Well you should know. If this was a mining area, you'd know all about the local mills. This probably lasted longer and handled more wealth than any of them."

Tully just shrugged, but while Wendy was setting up her equipment he drifted to where an elderly woman was watering a desperate lawn at one of the few houses still occupied.

When they got back in the car Tully said, "I don't know exactly when it was built, but it shut down back in the early fifties. The town has never recovered, according to that woman over there. Trains don't stop here any more, her husband used to maintain the tracks. Lots of trains still use them, carrying container cars from China. They just blast on by. Did you get any photos?"

"I did. Did you get the woman's name and exact information for your dissertation?"

"I did. I'll be able to find more, exact dates and stuff, at the archives in Santa Fe."

#

Wendy's mood improved upon learning that Tully had actually gathered useful information, so she said, "Let's go to Pleasant Valley, show Samster where we hit it big gambling at the Senior Center."

As they drove, Tully thought about that night. It seemed long ago. It had been one of the happiest times he and Wendy had had together, laughing about the prizes they won, planning to cook the beans she'd won, the people they met who had driven miles for a bingo game. Interviewing Wilbur Frost together.

Now he and Wendy barely spoke. Now Crazy Tony was a bigger presence in his life than Wendy was. How could he have been so stupid?

#

"Looks like the big parade was yesterday," quipped Samster as they drove the highway through the comatose village. "Too bad we missed it."

"Actually, they do have a parade, once a year," said Tully. "They call it Old Home Day, when anyone who's ever lived here comes back to the Old Home. I read about it up in the archives. From the photos, it's a pretty big deal."

Wendy remained silent.

They pulled in front of the community center. Tully, Samster, and Howdy got out. "Looks like we've missed the monthly bingo game too," said Tully. "I was counting on beans for dinner."

"I was counting on someone telling us where we could camp for the night," said Wendy.

The three looked around the village. No signs of life. They walked to the abandoned school, a large cement block building. Above the door was carved Pleasant Valley, 1937. A few windows still had glass in them; a single swing still hung in the playground.

"I was thinking of camping here," said Tully, pointing to what had once been a playground, "but I don't want to do it without telling someone."

At that moment from around the building an older man appeared. He wore an untucked green work shirt, faded jeans, and a weathered ball cap with the logo Surge Feeds on his head. By his side was a large husky-type dog. The man said, "Can I help you folks?"

"Yes, perhaps you can." After introductions Tully said, "We're friends of Grace and Henry and Vera and Elmer and the others who play bingo here at the community center. We also know Wilbur Frost."

"If you're here for the bingo, it isn't until next week." The man's scowl softened somewhat.

Wendy stepped forward. "The three of us are photographing and researching the history of the Estancia Valley, and we need a place to pitch our tents for the night. We were thinking the schoolyard would work. We have our own water and other facilities. All we need is to pitch our tents. We're very quiet."

"Then you should fit right in," the man said. "I'm Ralph Peppers, I'm the unofficial caretaker of the school. I don't see no harm in you camping here, but don't go in the building. We've had a problem with people going in and vandalizing, taking stuff as souvenirs. That school's on the historic register, built in 1937 by the WPA."

"And that would be?"

"Works Progress Administration. Part of the New Deal to get the country back working during the Depression."

"Poor old school," said Wendy. "It looks like it could use some work and progress now."

#

After setting up their tents, they drove on the highway south of Pleasant Valley to a dirt road and a sign pointing to Cedar Wells. Tully turned to Samster and Wendy. "At one time Cedar Wells was an important stop on the stage line between Santa Fe and the mining areas farther south."

"No minerals here?" asked Samster.

"Nope, just beans, but it was a lively place during the Bean Boom. I want to see the cemetery."

He told Samster and Wendy about Eduardo Duran. "It's not impossible he was on your family tree."

"Why not? Everyone else in New Mexico was."

"The cemetery should offer photographic possibilities," said Wendy.

"Oh, I'm sure it's just pulsating with poignancy," said Tully. Wendy glared at him.

#

Such buildings as remained in Cedar Wells were scattered widely over several acres. The wooden ones were falling apart, their boards weathered gray, though a few bore remnants of paint. The adobe buildings were dissolving in the infrequent rains. A few abandoned trailers lay tilted upon collapsing cinder-block foundations. A double-wide at the village's edge possibly was inhabited, though no vehicle was present.

Tully explained that the town had two cemeteries, one Protestant, the other Catholic. The cemetery with the words *Sagrada Familia* worked into its wrought iron gate was on a low ridge just east of what was left of a small chapel. They parked the car, then walked into the cemetery.

"We're looking for Duran," said Tully as they spread out.

Wendy began assembling her tripod. "Let's try to find the oldest grave—and the newest."

#

An hour later they were packing up. "How was the photography?" Samster asked Wendy.

She glanced at Tully, who was still inside the cemetery taking notes.

"Poignant. I was especially moved by the little jars that once held flowers, real or plastic, a long time ago. And the graves where the headstones were illegible, or missing. I saw one headstone where the only writing still visible said 'Beloved Mother.'"

"Did you notice how many children's graves there were?" asked Tully as he joined them. "Infant mortality was high then."

"And did you notice how many death dates correlated with the 1918 flu epidemic?" said Wendy.

"We found Durans," said Samster, "but not Eduardo."

"Wilbur Frost was right," said Wendy, "the epidemic wiped out the whole family. I don't know why Eduardo isn't here."

Tully looked at Samster, standing with uncharacteristic pensiveness looking at the graveyard. Perhaps some of those buried here had been Samster's ancestors. Tully knew that Samster had never been interested in his family's history, but looking at gravestones with your name on them can change one's perspective.

#

As they drove away, Samster looked again at the photos of Eduardo Duran that Tully had copied at the archives. Eduardo was perhaps younger than he was, but the somber face staring out from the photos was that of an adult. Eduardo was married, with children, raising a family, supporting them through hard work.

And he? A doper, a slacker, a flake, trying to get by doing as little as possible. Yes, he was responsible in a way for his family, but he was still living at home with his mother and little brother. He could no more imagine himself married with a family than he could imagine being Chinese.

And that bothered him. What would he be like in ten years? Twenty years? He'd known career stoners. He didn't want to be like them.

But he didn't know what to do.

If only he and Tully could find the Oro Mine.

#

They didn't talk as they drove back to Pleasant Valley. Wendy stopped twice to photograph abandoned homesteads. She tried to capture the heat waves rising from the parched soil.

At Pleasant Valley they unrolled their sleeping bags. As they were assembling their camp stoves Ralph Peppers appeared.

"I don't know what you've planned for supper, but I've got a pot of pork and beans in the house that's more than I can eat. You're welcome to share it."

"Are they local beans?" asked Samster.

"Wouldn't have any other."

Over dinner the man told them about growing up in Pleasant Valley, about the annual bean crop coming in, about drought, farms failing, businesses dying, and about the school closing. "Now me and a few other old-timers are all that's left. We're like the drying up puddles of the big lake that once was here."

Samster asked him about Eduardo Duran. "He was way before my time."

As they walked back to their tents, Wendy said, "I probably shouldn't mention this, but all day I've had the feeling of being watched."

"Funny you mention that," said Samster, "but I've had the same feeling."

"We should have brought Howdy as a guard dog," said Tully.

"That's not funny," said Wendy.

#

In the morning, after breakfast of bacon and eggs and beans with Ralph Peppers, they packed up.

"With the information I got from Mr. Peppers last night and the cemetery and the woman in that small town I'd count this trip a success," said Tully. "How about you two?"

Samster seemed preoccupied.

"I'm pleased with the photos I've taken," said Wendy. "I'd like to get more of the natural environment, the prairie grasses, that sort of thing."

"We should go to the salt lakes," said Samster. "I want to see the caves."

Wendy's mouth dropped. "No! Absolutely not! That's where someone shot at us." She looked at Tully for support. "You do remember that, don't you, Tully?"

Tully stood with his hands in the pockets of his jeans. Indecision clouded his face. Finally he said, "I'm with Samster. If we don't do it now, we'll do it later; that's just the way I am."

"But *why*?"

"It's hard to explain, but I just sense something out there is important."

"And you, Samster, you also have this mystical intuition that out in those wretched caves is something you just have to discover, like the Dead Sea Scrolls?"

Samster recoiled from her scorn. "Nah, I just want to explore the caves."

"So you refuse to go with us?" Tully asked.

"I wish," Wendy said, "but no, I'll drive you two out there because if I don't, you'll manage to get into worse trouble. But I'm not going to the caves. I'm staying in the car."

#

No one spoke as Wendy drove her little car over the two-track leading to the salt lakes. A thin scrim of high clouds dimmed the sunlight, muting the rich evening colors of their previous visit, but the subtle curves and colors of plains still fascinated Wendy. She thought of the abandoned homesteader cabins, the empty railroad silo, the graves at Cedar Wells, and the lined faces of Wilbur Frost and Ralph Peppers. Yes, she thought, this is what calls to me.

And it's at this that I excel, and I could become even better if I took classes, really pursued my craft, associated with other photographers.

Tully. He was no photographer, but he had an eye for details she sometimes overlooked, such as the significance of the World War II newspapers in the homestead's walls.

He also was unfailingly supportive. He'd do everything he could to encourage her career, regardless of how difficult and improbable it might seem. No, Tully was not one to let practicality be an obstacle to pursuing one's dreams. Not Tully, no, not Tully. That was why she'd broken up with Tully, his inability to factor practicality into his plans.

Now here she was, practical, sensible Wendy, with career prospects just as bleak as those of the two flakes, Samster and Tully.

So did she want to undo their breakup? Of course she did. She'd never doubted that. She belonged with Tully, but perhaps she belonged with Tully in ways she hadn't suspected. She tried to be reassured by that but didn't quite succeed.

#

When they approached the salt lakes they surveyed the landscape until they found a knoll that overlooked the area they'd be exploring. The salt flat was bone-white in the dull light. Along its eastern edge was a modest escarpment at whose base were several dark cracks and crevices.

"From here you can see the whole area," Samster remarked. "Doesn't look like anyone's here. Or at least they're well-concealed."

"Thanks," said Wendy, "that really reassures me. I still have this creepy feeling we're being watched."

From inside her car Wendy looked on as Tully and Samster descended to the salt flat, then walked toward the caves. Both carried flashlights from their camping kits. Cautiously they approached one of the larger caves, examined its opening, then entered.

Frustrated by waiting, Wendy got out of the car, retrieved a telephoto lens from her photographic equipment, screwed it onto a camera, then attached it to a tripod. With this she had a much better view of the caves.

After what felt like a long time but probably was only ten minutes the two emerged. Samster, seeing her watching them, waved. She waved back.

Then the two entered the next cave. They were in longer this time. Again Samster waved when they emerged.

The third cave they entered was the largest. After half an hour of waiting Wendy was getting apprehensive. She considered getting into the car and driving down when she heard a vehicle. Across the salt flat a pickup was raising a plume of white dust. It stopped at the entrance to the cave containing Tully and Samster and a man got out. He was carrying a rifle.

#

"This looks more complex than the other caves," said Samster as he shone his flashlight on the cave's pale white walls, occasionally catching the gleam of calcite crystals. On the cave's rough floor were twigs, cholla stalks and fruit, juniper branches—debris brought in by packrats.

Small tunnels branched from the main one. Steadily they probed deeper, the passages getting narrower, the ceilings lower.

Suddenly Samster exclaimed, "Whoa! Check this out!" He shined his flashlight onto a low ledge in an inconspicuous side cave.

Resting on the ledge was a mass of old juniper branches, placed there deliberately. And protruding from the mass were the bones of a human arm.

"Holy crap!" Tully gasped as he crept closer. Neither wanted to touch the skeleton, but they forced themselves to get a closer look. They could see other bones among the branches and even part of the skull. And judging from the scraps of clothing still clinging to the bones the body was not that of an ancient Indian.

For a long time they could only stare. Finally Samster said, "This creeps me out, let's get out of here. We need to tell someone about this."

They emerged breathless from the cave to find Wendy shouting at them as she raced across the salt flat—and a man pointing a rifle at them. It was Wilbur Frost.

Wilbur was the only one able to speak.

"You found it, didn't you."

Tully turned to Wendy, whose eyes were wide with terror. "We found a skeleton in the cave," he said. Then turning to Wilbur he said, "That's what you meant, isn't it?"

Wilbur just nodded, then said, "I tried to encourage you to stay away, but you wouldn't do it, and now you dumb young 'uns solved a mystery that a couple of generations of local people couldn't solve. You found Oscar Bollinger."

"Wha ... what?" muttered Tully.

"That was you shooting at us?" said Wendy.

"Shooting near you. If I'd really been shooting at you, you wouldn't be here now."

"But why?" said Tully. "I thought you and your brother looked for him when he disappeared and didn't find him."

"Tom looked for him. I knew where he was. I'd killed him."

Wendy's eyes shifted back and forth from Frost's grim face and the gun he held. "Are ... are you going to kill us?"

Frost looked at her, then at the other two. Then he lowered the gun. "Of course not. I'm not a murderer. I didn't intend to kill Bollinger. I'm not going to shoot three innocent young people to cover up a sixty-year-old killing."

He lowered the gun, and looked at them. Wendy saw sadness and resignation in his eyes. Then he told them the story:

"All us kids in the area were obsessed by Oscar Bollinger. He was an eccentric old coot, all kinds of legends and stories swirled around him, especially stories of him having magical beans and money stashed away. He was a recluse, anyone who tried to get near his place he'd run 'em off with a gun, shot at kids with a shotgun and bird shot. But that only reinforced our conviction that he was like Long John Silver, with treasure squirreled away out here in these salt flats.

"I lived closer to him than the other kids, so one day when I seen him saddle up his horse and ride out this way I resolved to follow him. I was a pretty good tracker, from rounding up cattle strays, and I was able to keep out of sight as he went here. I hunkered down and watched him go into that cave you just came out of. When he didn't come out for a long time I crept closer and waited. I had my .22 rifle with me; I never went anywhere without it, because of rattlesnakes and such.

"As I hunkered there by the entrance he suddenly appeared behind me, pointing his gun at me. He'd come out of one of the other caves. He looked wild, crazy. "I'll teach you to try to steal what's mine," he shouted, and he raised his gun.

I dived for the ground as he got off a shot, and through pure instinct I shot back with my .22. I didn't aim, I just shot. I hit him square in the forehead.

"No doubt he was dead. I was terrified. I didn't know what to do. I'd just killed a man. I was trembling and crying. Finally I dragged his body back into the cave, found a ledge deep in one of the side-passages, and put him there. Then over the next few days I brought in juniper branches and covered him up.

"Bollinger didn't have any relatives, and while people knew he'd disappeared, looked for him, no one missed him. I always intended to come clean and tell people what happened, but I never did, and the years rolled by.

"And then you young 'uns come along. Now I expect I'll be talking to the sheriff and lawyers and the county attorney. No one can dispute that it was self-defense, and though I'm definitely guilty of some offenses I won't go to prison, not at my age and after all this time. But my life will become much more complicated, what with all the publicity. I figured I'd just live out my days here, and maybe leave a written statement after I was gone."

Tully looked at Wendy and Samster, then said, "I can't speak for them, but I think that's what you should do."

"That's exactly what you should do," declared Samster.

"I don't see any compelling reason why we should say anything to anyone," added Wendy.

The old man looked at the three, then said, "That's kind of you."

As he started to turn away Tully said, "There is something you can do for us, or for me, at least. As you know, I'm working on my dissertation on the early bean economy in the Estancia Valley—and to be honest I'm not making much progress. I'm about to be kicked out of the program. One problem is I just can't get a handle on it.

"Would you consent to spending serious time with me talking in detail about what it was like then? I'd like to record you, and Wendy is making a photographic record of the early days for my dissertation. Talking to you would give me the personal, human perspective that I've been looking for."

Frost looked hard at Tully. "As you know, I'm not big on visitors, but I've had worse ones than you, and I certainly would rather talk to you than the sheriff and the lawyers. I'll do it. You know where to find me."

As Frost turned to walk away Tully said, "I've got another request, a small one." From his backpack he retrieved the plastic freezer bag in which he kept the Oro map. He handed the map to Frost.

"Tully!" Wendy started to say, but it was too late.

Tully continued. "You said you used to herd cattle all around this country. We've got a map showing mountains we can't identify. Could you look at it and see if you recognize them?"

The old man peered at the map. "I can't make out the writing, but, sure, I recognize those mountains. That one peak with the cat's ears is Panther Peak. That's in the

Sierra del Sombre. Me and other cowboys used to round up strays in the foothills. It's rough, lonely, dangerous country."

Once more Frost turned away but this time was interrupted by Samster. "When you went into the cave, did you find the money Bollinger supposedly stashed in there?"

Frost snorted. "I did. It was $53 in moldy bills. That was a fair piece of change in those days, but I left it there. I'm sure it's lining a packrat nest by now.

"Some treasure. That's how it is with those things. They have a way of looking great and glamorous from far off and then shrinking the closer you get until they disappear altogether when you actually get to them, but lusting for them can make you walk right off a cliff—like it did with me."

CHAPTER 23

Tully knocked on the jamb of the open door before entering Elnora's office. She arched her eyebrows as she looked up from the papers she was reading. "Hello, Tully."

Tully savored the confidence he felt as he placed a manila folder on her desk. "There's the outline you requested. I also wanted to give you a verbal progress report."

"Yes?"

"I've made another trip to Bean Country." He told her about getting information about the railroad silo, about interviewing Ralph Peppers at the school, visiting the Cedar Wells cemetery, and Wendy's photographs.

"And best of all Wilbur Frost, one of the few remaining old-time bean farmers, has agreed to extensive interviews about his experiences. I think it's coming together. I'm pretty excited about it."

"Tully, that's wonderful. I could use good news."

Tully lowered himself into the chair in front of Elnora's desk. "I need to do more work in the archives in Santa Fe, but I know that will be easier now that I've met Roland. He's eager to help with this project."

"If you have Roland helping you, you're half-way there. Did you have anything else?" Elnora asked.

It sounded to Tully like Elnora was eager to get rid of him. "No, that's it. I just wanted to impart good news, for a change."

"I'm happy for you, I really am. It's just that this is a difficult time in the department. Dorothy Liggon has announced her retirement, and Spencer has been pushing to have Kenzie Yates for her replacement."

"What?!" Tully's mouth gaped. "Kenzie Yates to replace Dorothy Liggon? That's like naming Britney Spears to replace Eleanor Roosevelt."

Elnora tried to stifle a laugh, didn't succeed.

Tully leaned forward. "I know I shouldn't be snarky about a faculty member, but among history students, undergraduate and graduate alike, she's an airhead. I took her seminar about gender roles in Walt Disney's films, thinking the subject had potential, but all she talked about were Cinderella and Snow White and the handsome prince to the rescue trope. I don't think she'd ever heard of Tinkerbell or Bambi's mother."

Tully chose not to mention the common knowledge among students that Kenzie and Spencer had become more than just colleagues; he assumed Elnora already knew that.

Still laughing Elnora said, "Dammit Tully, I was really enjoying my bad mood until you came along. But seriously, if Spencer succeeds in this, the whole department will suffer. Already morale is at an all-time low. Other faculty have been talking about retiring or leaving."

"I hope that doesn't include you."

Elnora hesitated. "I won't deny that I'm pretty frustrated here. But don't worry. I'll keep you informed of any decisions I make—and I won't throw you overboard." She paused, then laughed, "Not now that you're finally getting serious. I'm dying to see what a focused Tully would look like."

#

After Tully left Elnora tried to return to the papers on her desk but instead found herself staring at the map of the western US on her wall. She recalled what Dorothy Liggon had said announcing her retirement. "There are places of historical significance I've always wanted to visit, beautiful old libraries whose collections I've wanted to explore, scholars I've wanted to meet—and if I don't leave now I never will."

Elnora thought of Kalyssa Santiago, her friend from graduate school, now vice-chair of the history department at Summit College in central Colorado. They'd been close as students, and had kept in touch. She'd been the first person Elnora had told that Spencer wasn't really the person he projected to be. More than once Kalyssa had suggested that Elnora consider applying for a position at Summit. It was a small school, far beneath the state university in status, and the salary was comparably lower as well.

Still, it was located in an attractive Colorado mountain town, near the San Juan Mountains, close to the places of western history Elnora yearned to study. Initially it had been a difficult decision.

But Elnora had achieved tenure at the state university, which was far above Summit in prestige and the ability to attract students and grants, she loved her house near campus, and she liked her students and colleagues, with only the normal proportion of exceptions. To leave for the smaller school would be career self-mutilation.

Now, however ...

#

As Samster walked across campus after leaving Tully, he thought about Tully and himself. They'd been best friends since elementary school, partners in countless adventures, confidants in dozens of personal crises. They'd partied together, smoked a lot of dope together.

Yet here was Tully meeting with his academic adviser, and he was walking to his part-time job at a bicycle shop. He'd never begrudged Tully being more academically talented, because he had talents of his own. He regarded renovating and fixing bicycles as having as much social value as studying history.

And again images and thoughts of Eduardo Duran returned, as they had so often since visiting Cedar Wells. Why had he become almost an obsession? A poor young man who'd disappeared almost a century ago. A poor young man who wasn't really much different from himself—except culture, language, religion, upbringing, family ... Just what did he and Eduardo have in common? Why did he feel a connection to him?

Since the trip to Bean Country Samster had taken a sabbatical from Wobbling Wally's to avoid encountering Tony. He'd told his friends there to say they thought Samster had gone to North Dakota if Tony came by to ask.

He'd told his mother and Elron to say the same thing, and he'd learned that in fact Tony had come by his house asking about him. He'd talked to Elron, who had managed to be especially opaque in that manner unique to adolescent nerdy males. Samster was proud of Elron.

#

Attorney Estella Mondragon leaned forward over her desk and continued scribbling on the legal pad in front of her. Wendy thought, I hate it when lawyers do that. Finally she looked up. "I have good news, and bad news."

"Can I choose which I hear first?" Wendy asked.

"I'll give you the bad news first." She paused. "I've been in touch with the administrators at the school. They're trying desperately to minimize their liability and also any negative publicity that might ensue from this case. They've concluded that part of that strategy will be to terminate you."

Wendy sat stolidly. When she said nothing the lawyer continued. "This decision hasn't officially been made yet. They'll notify you in writing, and you'll have recourse to an appeals process, in which I'll be happy to represent you, but I'm afraid it will be long, nasty, and expensive—with only slight hope of success."

"Don't contest it."

"What?"

"I don't want to fight it. If it will help, I'll resign."

The lawyer was nonplussed. "Resigning might be better than being fired, but either will make finding another position extremely problematic."

"Don't contest it," Wendy repeated. "It's time I found a new career. Now, what's the good news?"

"Eli's parents, the Kleins, have been aggressively pursuing their suit against the Bendermans, and during their investigations they've uncovered evidence showing just what a nasty little sadist Brendan really is."

"Such as? Everyone at the school knew what he was like."

"It turns out his neighbors also know what he's like. He has a reputation for torturing neighborhood pets. He used a lighter to burn a kitten. He's also accused of setting fires in the neighborhood. He's a perfect example of a sadistic psychopath in the making."

Wendy's eyes widened. "I didn't know this, but I'm not surprised."

"No one, not even the Bendermans, knew the true extent of this kid's viciousness, and suffice it to say they're not eager to have it all exposed at trial. And it will make it much easier to portray you as rescuer rather than perpetrator.

"None of this is particularly good news for the school, which did nothing to protect the students from this little predator, but it is good news for your defense."

Wendy nodded.

"This doesn't mean the Bendermans will drop their suits against the school—or you—but things have become much more complicated for them, and for us that's good news.

"In the meantime, the investigations will continue, motions will be filed. Nothing will happen soon, these things move slowly. If you leave town, let me know how I can reach you."

As Wendy rose to leave attorney Mondragon said, "Are you sure you don't want to challenge your termination? Increasingly you come across as having done the right thing. We'd have a strong case."

"Thanks, but no. I'm clear about this. Nasty little Brendan might have done me a favor."

#

Elnora was still at her desk staring at the map when she heard heavy footsteps outside her office door. She looked up at a burly, unshaven man with dark, glowering eyes.

"I'm looking for a kid named Tully. They told me downstairs you were his teacher."

"I'm his adviser, if that's what you mean."

"Whatever," the man growled as he stepped into the office.

When he left a few minutes later Elnora with shaking hands scrabbled through her rolodex file until she found Tully's cell phone number.

"Tully, I need to speak with you—now."

CHAPTER 24

Samster was distraught when he met Tully and Wendy at the university's student union building, his hands shaking.

"We've got to do something—and now! This can't go on."

"What's wrong?" asked Wendy.

"Tony went to my house and roughed up Elron, broke a couple of computers. Elron was in tears when I came home. He's not seriously hurt, but he's just a kid. He's pretty traumatized, not to mention the loss of the computers—which weren't his."

"What did Elron tell Tony?" asked Tully.

"The truth: he didn't know where I was or when I'd be home. Tony said he'd be back if he didn't find me soon. This can't go on. What if it had been my mom?"

"No, this can't go on," said Tully. He told them about Tony going to the history department and confronting Elnora.

"What did she do?" asked Wendy.

"Same as Elron: said she didn't know where I was. She threatened to call campus security, but he just smirked as if that was the least of his concerns. She was pretty shaken up. We've got to do something. Sooner or later he'll find one of us, and in the meantime he's a menace to everyone we know."

Wendy pursed her lips, then shook her head.

"What?" asked Samster.

"I was thinking it's time to involve the authorities, get a restraining order—and I think that's still a good idea—but Tony got the jump on us. By the time we set the legal procedures in motion—restraining order, revoking probation, all that—it could be too late." She shook her head.

"I think what we should do is obvious," said Samster with uncharacteristic certainty. "We should find the mine."

"What?!" exclaimed Wendy. "Are you out of your freaking mind? That's supposed to get Tony off our tail? Looking for that stupid mine and finding it, assuming that's even possible, is the worst thing we could do. That's like trying to get rid of a vicious dog by holding a steak."

Tully gave Samster a skeptical look. "I guess I need to hear your reasoning."

"Oh for heaven's sake," said Wendy. "I can't believe we're even considering this. Every time you two come up with a way to shake Tony—looking for a pyrite sample, buying one in a rock shop—we just toss him a bone that keeps him on the chase. The real answer is obvious. We give him the rock and the map, he goes away on what almost certainly is a wild goose chase, and we get back to our lives. Do we really think we're going to wake up one morning to newspaper headlines reading 'Socorro Man Finds Missing Mine, Suddenly Wealthy'. It never happens. Tully, you know that, don't you?"

Tully nodded, but he continued looking at Samster.

"What's my reasoning? Actually it's based on what Wendy just said. What if it is just a wild goose chase? We find the mine, and it turns out to be a bunch of fool's gold. Or more likely we don't find the mine, in which case we give the map to Tony and wish him luck. Whatever happens we're keeping the rock."

"Sure," said Wendy, "crazy treasure hunters like you two and Tony and everyone looking for the Lost Dutchman and the Lost Adams Diggings and all the rest—they're just famous for giving up when at first they don't find the treasure. Bullshit! They spend the rest of their miserable, wasted lives looking for it. They assume they didn't read the map right, or they assume they went up the wrong draw, or it's just over the ridge, right there at the end of the rainbow."

For the first time, Tully looked at Wendy before turning again to Samster. "I'm afraid Wendy's right on this. Treasure hunters don't give up. If the Lost Dutchman seekers found a little pit with a bottle containing a note from the Dutchman himself saying, 'April Fools! I made it all up,' they'd just keep searching.

"But Samster does have a point. Tony's not going to give up until he has the rock and the map."

"But Tony doesn't know we have a map," said Wendy. "Unless you told him." She aimed her gaze at Samster.

"No, we didn't," Samster replied, "but he knows we've been following up on something, and he'll know the rock didn't come from the Chupaderas and we didn't find it just out hiking. He won't be satisfied with just the rock.

"And besides, as I've said before, we're not giving him the rock."

"I'm with Samster," said Tully. Wendy frowned. "We either give him everything—or we give him nothing. And dammit, giving into his intimidation is wrong. In the Old

West he'd have been branded a claim jumper—and probably strung up."

"So you're saying we should go to the Sierra del Sombre with that ridiculous map and try to find the mine?" asked Wendy.

"I guess that is what I am saying," said Samster. "I admit it sounds as risky and self-defeating to me as it does to you—well, almost—but this has to come to a resolution. We've got to stop being on the run and it's time we took the initiative."

Wendy sagged, defeated. Tully went and put his arm around her. "I'm really scared," she choked, trying to hold back tears. "I've tried to be up and rational about all this, despite the insanity I see before my eyes from you two. But the last incidents involving Tony Kalvari have shown me that this isn't just a Hardy Boys Whiz-bang adventure. I don't want anyone to get hurt."

"Wendy, I've had the same thoughts," said Tully, "and if that's how you feel, then we're not going. But I have to warn you: the allure of lost treasure doesn't die easily." They both looked at Samster.

"I'll vote with Tully, and you, Wendy. But not even a skateboard slacker would believe that turning around will be the last of the Oro—or Crazy Tony. If we want rid of him, sooner or later we have to give him the map."

Wendy scowled, shook her head, then shrugged her shoulders. "So we're going treasure hunting. After all the distractions and problems and fear that treasure hunting has caused us, we're going to resolve it by going treasure hunting."

Tully looked at Wendy. "You don't have to go. *We* don't have to go. You're an innocent bystander in all this."

With her mouth grim she looked at Tully, then at Samster. "No I'm not. For better or for worse, we're in this together. Besides, this foolhardy expedition should include at least one functioning brain cell."

"Then we need to move fast," said Samster. "For all we know Tony will walk through those doors"—he gestured with his head at the student union's entrance—"as we're sitting here." Instantly both Tully and Wendy looked at the doors, then back at Samster.

"And we need to leave a cover story, like with Elron and my mom and the people at Wobbling Wally's and Elnora."

"I've got it," said Tully. "We'll say we're going on a camping trip into the Black Range." Wendy looked with concern at him. Was he enjoying this?

"There's dacite there," he continued, "and there was mineralization and mining."

"We can say we're looking for the Lost Adams Diggings," said Samster. He too seemed to be getting into this, in an unhealthy way.

"Come on, you two," she said, "this isn't a game of hide-and-seek. This is deadly serious."

"Wendy's right," said Tully. "Let's just say we're going camping in the Black Range. Tony can draw his own conclusions."

#

For the rest of the day they scurried around, gathering their backpacking gear and planting the cover story. Elnora appeared skeptical, but she agreed when Tully insisted it was what she should tell Tony should he reappear. Samster told Elron and his mother to try to avoid

Tony, if possible, but if not to tell them the Black Range story. He did the same at the bicycle shop.

At day's end they met again at the student union. "We're ready to leave at first light," said Tully.

"No," said Samster, "we should leave *now*. I don't want to leave us exposed here even overnight. We should get out *now*. I'll bet Crazy Tony has been watching us."

Wendy was taken aback by Samster's urgency but remembered that his brother had been roughed up by Tony. "Yes, we should go now. You two get together whatever you need, I'll do the same, then we'll meet here in an hour. We'll drive to the movie theater, go in, then after half an hour we'll leave and return to our car. We have nothing to gain and everything to lose by hanging around here overnight. We can stay at a motel in Socorro and make plans for tomorrow."

"Wow," said Tully. "You make this sound like a spy novel."

"I'm with Wendy," Samster said. "Remember that Tony had no trouble finding where we lived."

Sobered, Tully agreed. "Let's not let dawn find us in Albuquerque."

"It's not dawn we have to worry about," said Samster.

CHAPTER 25

They spent a sleepless night in cheap motel near
Socorro, Wendy in the bed, Tully and Samster in sleeping
bags on the floor. A storm was approaching from the west;
every time the wind blew a piece of debris across the
parking lot outside, Samster got up and looked out the
window. Tully had scoffed, but was shut down by stern
looks from Wendy and Samster. They were right; one of
his failings always had been a refusal to accept that bad
things really did happen.

They arose before dawn, scanned the motel parking lot,
and then, seeing nothing suspicious, grabbed a quick
breakfast at a fast food place. Now they sat in Wendy's
little Honda as she drove the highway in the direction of
the Sierra del Sombre. Tully sat in the passenger seat,
maps spread upon his lap. Samster in the back.

Samster kept turning to look at the road behind them.
"Would you quit doing that," Wendy barked. "You're
making me nervous."

"You'd be a lot more nervous if Tony's pickup suddenly
appeared behind us."

Wendy just shrugged.

"Yep, this is the right road, this is the only paved road
for fifty miles," quipped Tully, trying to ease the tension.

His joke fell flat; he stared out the window. The terrain
on both sides was a bare-earth wasteland of hills and

ridges and gullies; only a few struggling junipers, tough shrubs, and grasses could live among the jagged rocks scattered like shrapnel from a colossal explosion. The rocks' colors—red, orange, gray, and black—were reminiscent of the slag around smelters.

Ahead the hazy outlines of mountain ranges floated like mirages in the dry, dusty desert air. Somewhere to the southwest was the ancient Spanish wagon route called the Jornada del Muerto, the "Journey of the Dead Man," for a traveler, one of many, who had not survived the dangerous passage.

"Can we see the Sierra del Sombre from here?" asked Samster.

"I'm not sure," said Tully. "They could be those peaks to the south, but it's hard to tell. We should know as we get closer. Are you in a hurry?"

Samster didn't answer. Last night in the motel, while Tully and Wendy had hunkered over the maps and tried to plot a route, he'd used Tully's laptop to seek information about the Sierra del Sombre. They were a small range, overshadowed by larger ranges nearby, but they were compact and distinct, a dark, gnarly knot of volcanic rocks in the linear skein of limestone ridges to the north and south.

No one knew the origin of the name. Perhaps it derived from the "Mountains of the Shadow" being "overshadowed" by adjacent larger ranges. Perhaps it came from the darkness of its volcanic rocks. One source suggested it translated a Mescalero Apache Indian name for the mountains, who avoided it because of its dark reputation in their myths.

Everyone else had avoided them too. No minerals had

been discovered in them, ranchers scorned them, stage routes avoided them.

Yet an old prospector had gone into them and in an anonymous canyon found or did something that caused him to write the word *Oro* on a crude map.

Oro. Gold. And he, Samster, had actually seen it glittering in the rock he'd found in the Chupaderas, a rock that hadn't come from there. Gold. Until that rock, gold had been a mere abstraction to him, something that governments possessed, that people used to make jewelry, a symbol, a color. But now he had held it in his hand, it was *his*. And if he possessed more of it his life would change.

But it was the thought of just having it that most excited him. While Wendy and Tully talked as they drove he reached into his backpack and took out the rock. Just holding it gave him an odd sense of pride. Tully had talked about the apparent contradiction of people like the Dutchman living in poverty while possessing a mine of untold riches, but Samster understood how the gold wasn't just something like coins to purchase other things, it was the prize unto itself. Just seeing it, holding it, gave him pleasure. Giving up the rock to Tony, or anyone, was unthinkable.

"I see them," said Tully after almost an hour. "That's the Sierra del Sombre." He pointed to a cluster of jagged peaks to the southeast. He took his binoculars and peered ahead. "I think I can see Panther Peak. Here, take a look."

Samster squinted his eyes, then made out what with a little imagination resembled the twin ears of a cat. "Yeah, I think that's it. How do we get there?"

"Most of the land here is privately owned by ranchers," said Tully, "except for a strip of land leading to the Sierra del Sombre. The mountains themselves are owned by the U.S. Bureau of Land Management. That means it's our land, except that much of the range is within White Sands Missile Range.

"Apparently the land was so worthless even ranchers didn't bother to claim it. The maps show a small road leading to a stock tank. From there it's hiking, but the tank isn't far from the canyon that Wendy and I think might be the one shown on Toler's map."

"Sounds simple," said Samster.

Wendy, who had been silent, snorted a scoffing laugh.

#

"I think we missed it," said Tully as their car continued east on the paved road. "We should turn around."

As they drove back Wendy said, "Could that be it?" She pointed to two wooden fence posts out of step with others lining the highway. They pulled over and found a crude gate.

"If this is public land," asked Samster, "why is it fenced?"

"It's our land, but ranchers lease it to graze cattle, and they don't want their animals wandering onto the highway."

Tully undid the wire fastenings of the gate, then Wendy drove through while Samster held it open. Afterward he fastened the gate shut again."

As he walked back to the car he looked at the ground. "Doesn't look like this 'road' gets much traffic. Like none."

Tully pulled up a scrubby snakeweed plant and brushed the track to obscure their tire prints. A pathetic attempt but better than nothing.

"The road just goes to the stock tank, and I haven't seen any cattle since we've been driving, so there's no reason for anyone to be here."

"My poor little car," moaned Wendy as she steered it over the vague track strewn with rocks. Saltbush and snakeweed in the road's center scuffed the car's undercarriage.

After two miles of three-miles-an-hour driving they arrived at a decrepit aluminum stock tank, connected by a pipe to a non-functioning windmill. No recent cattle tracks surrounded the tank.

They parked the car and unloaded their gear. "Be sure to turn off all the lights," said Samster. "If we had a dead battery out here no one would come by with jumper cables." Each drank as much water as their stomachs would hold from gallon water jugs in the car's trunk.

The sun was nearing noon when they hoisted their packs.

\#

The twin cat ears of Panther Peak loomed ahead as they hiked toward a deep, narrow canyon leading into the mountains. Yesterday's storm was upon them, blowing dust and threatening rain from dark clouds. Only Samster was in good spirits as they followed what appeared to be a faint animal trail. At the canyon's mouth it disappeared among boulders and bushes. They set their packs down and rested in the shade of an overhanging ledge, sipping from their water bottles.

"What are we looking for?" asked Samster.

"If this is the canyon shown on the map we'll follow it

into the mountains. Both Toler's map and the topographic map show a spring in the canyon bottom about a mile in. We'll look for that first. Then we'll look for side canyons. We're looking for one that bends sharply east."

"Well, that sure narrows it down," muttered Wendy. "I'll bet they all bend toward the east, though I recall the topographic map showing a canyon with a distinct elbow near its mouth. Do you suppose we'll see any trail signs, like cairns?"

"Won't hurt to look," said Tully.

"Look at this," Samster said as they hoisted their packs. He pointed to a large arrowhead half-buried in the soil. He knelt and picked it up. It was made of dark-red chert, its tip broken.

"That would have been a pretty hefty arrow to carry this," said Samster.

"Probably not an arrow but a dart, thrown by an atlatl, a spear thrower. They were used by ancient Indians, before bows and arrows. That makes it really old, anywhere from three to eight thousand years old, maybe older. If there's no other artifacts around, perhaps the dart went into an animal who then escaped. The animal carried it around until it died. Maybe the animal was a mammoth, or a saber-toothed tiger."

"Whoa!" said Samster. "Should I keep it?"

"I wouldn't," said Tully. "Let's photograph it, then put it back, maybe cover it up, or protect it with a rock."

Wendy took it from Samster and examined it. "Well, this also means we're not the first humans here, though I hope we don't wind up like this beast."

#

Boulders and debris made the hiking slow in the canyon's bottom. Tully pointed to branches and limbs tangled in rocks above them. "That's a bad sign," said Tully. "Those were left by a flash flood that surged down the canyon. This canyon with its steep walls would be a death trap for anyone caught here during a flood."

They all glanced upward at the storm clouds overhead, but so far they'd felt no precipitation.

Wendy normally enjoyed hiking, especially with Tully and Samster, but she had only bad feelings about this hike. Not only was it for all the wrong reasons, but the mountains themselves exhibited none of the beauty and peace she normally found in wild nature.

Rather, these mountains appeared hostile, even malevolent. No water, nothing truly green, the sparse vegetation designed for hoarding moisture and defending it. Prickly pear cacti, barrel cacti, catclaw acacia, agaves with spear-point leaves that could punch through cloth, ocotillo with leafless wand-like stalks whose spines evoked medieval scourges.

Whenever she began to relax she'd glimpse in the corner of her eye a soap tree yucca on a ridge, and her calm would be shattered by perceiving for the briefest of instants not a plant but a human watcher.

Dry and gnarly. The canyon was narrow, and cramped. No wonder humans had avoided these mountains.

Wendy didn't want to be here, and she noted that even Tully and Samster were subdued, without their usual banter and jokes. She wanted this expedition to be over. She wanted them to find nothing. No, she wanted more than nothing; she wanted something that would convince

Tully and Samster that there was no mine, that it didn't exist. She didn't know what that might be, but she didn't want them to go away thinking it was out here, that they simply hadn't found it. She wanted it to die, once and for all.

#

"I think this might have been the spring," said Tully. He pointed to the skeleton of a long-dead cottonwood, its gray, leafless branches lying naked in the sand. Nearby was a ledge bearing white stains from calcium-laden water that once had trickled over it.

"Some spring," humphed Samster. "Glad we didn't count on that for water."

"These mountains really haul out the welcome wagon, don't they," said Wendy.

"This spring probably had a lot of water when the ancient Indians were here," said Tully.

Wendy just shook her head.

Tully dug into the sand at the ledge's base. Despite digging over two feet the sand remained dry.

Then they resumed hiking up the canyon.

They passed several small side canyons, but none matched the canyon with the crook shown on the maps, and none showed any signs of anyone ever having been in them. Tully examined the rocks in the canyon bottoms; none resembled the rock in Samster's backpack.

As the sun was about to set they came to a larger side canyon that looked like it could be the one on the maps. Tully got out his compass and tried to triangulate exactly where they were. "I'm not really good at this, but I picked up a little from my dad on our rock-hounding expeditions. If this is the canyon on the topo map, Panther Peak should be about fifteen degrees to the northeast—and that's what the compass shows."

"Let's camp here and explore it in the morning," said Wendy, "when we're fresh. I'm exhausted."

Just inside the side canyon was a bench with enough room for their tents. "Would this bench be above flood level if the storm had a cloudburst in it?" asked Wendy.

Tully looked at the narrow canyon and its steep walls. "'Fraid not."

"At the first sign of rain or thunder or lightning we should start climbing," suggested Samster. "It would be tough going, but we should be able to get part of the way above the bottom."

Tully frowned. "Sorry, but we could be hit by a flash flood and never know it was coming, never see a drop of rain—if the rain fell far upstream. All we'd see would be a wall of water barreling down on us, and by the time we saw or heard it would be too late."

"Great!" said Wendy, "More cheerful news. So what do we do, sit here and play flash flood roulette?"

#

They scrambled around the canyon's slopes until finally Tully found a cramped but relatively level place. "This looks to be above the debris line from the last flash flood. We'll sleep with our feet pointed slightly downhill, but this is the best we've come up with, unless we want to go explore a little more."

"No thanks," said Wendy. "My feet don't mind pointing

downhill as long as I'm not standing on them."

They set up their tents, then returned to the canyon bottom. Wendy sat on a rock and rested, but Tully and Samster were oddly energized.

I'm finally here, thought Tully. I'm finally on a real lost treasure hunt. Too bad Crazy Tony has to be involved to spoil the romance and excitement, but I'm finally here, following an old map into a desert range to find something that inspired an old prospector to write *Oro* on the map. There's something here, I just *know* it.

After spending much of his life reading about lost treasures, and concluding that almost all were just folklore, he finally was a participant. Maybe this too would prove to be just a fantasy, but at the moment they had more evidence that it was real than that it was not. They had the map, which no one else had followed, so no one else had tried and failed to find the *Oro*, unlike the thousands of frustrated searchers for the Lost Dutchman Mine.

And they had the gold-bearing rock. If ever a lost mine could be real, it could be this one. They had no proof the rock had come from the Sierra del Sombre, but it was not an unreasonable deduction. If they found the mine, there'd be more gold, and then ...

And then?

As he stood in the mouth of a canyon that might actually hold a lost gold mine, Tully suddenly realized that in all his treasure-hunting fantasies he'd never thought about what would happen the day *after* he found the lost mine. Would the gold be in the form of nuggets? Or tiny flecks in a matrix of other rocks? Or, as with most gold mines, as invisible granules measured in ounces per ton of worthless rock?

And how would they convert the metal in the rocks into cash? What equipment would they need to extract the ore? Would they need to build a road to the mine? How would they go about filing a claim, if that was even allowed. And what about smelting? He was pretty sure the BLM wouldn't allow them just to go in and start hauling out gold-bearing rocks. What were current government regulations regarding that? And then selling the bullion? How would they deal with land-ownership issues?

Tully had never considered any of those details, because for him treasure-hunting had never been about actually finding treasure and converting it to spendable currency. No, treasure-hunting was about the romance, the mysteries, the searching. All those would end if they found the mine. What remained would be the chores and practicalities of the kind he'd struggled all his life to avoid.

So did he really want to find the mine? Of course, that moment of discovery was the prize that drove the game. Peering into the mine shaft or adit, seeing the glint of gold—that would be the ineffable victory, like reaching the top of a previously unclimbed mountain.

But for the first time, Tully realized that everything after that moment would be anticlimax.

#

"Look," said Samster, as the three explored the junction of the two canyons. He held aloft a spent rifle cartridge. Its tarnished metal showed it had been on the ground a long time. "At least one person's been here since our prehistoric mammoth hunter."

The three examined it, then returned it to the ground. Samster and Tully explored the side canyon's mouth while Wendy picked her way up the main canyon.

Suddenly she screamed.

Tully and Samster dashed toward her.

"Look!" She pointed to a large rattlesnake coiled on the sand. Its raised tail was vibrating angrily, the sound of the rattles almost like a hiss. Its broad, heart-shaped head was arched back into its coils, tense and poised.

"Whoa!" exclaimed Samster as he circled it.

"I almost stepped on it," gasped Wendy. "Another step and I would have. If I'd been distracted ..."

"It's a western diamondback," said Tully as he approached.

"Get away!" shouted Wendy.

"I'm okay," he said. "They can't strike beyond two-thirds of their body's length, and they rarely strike at all. This is a big one, over four feet, but I'm safe if I stay at least five feet away. My dad and I encountered a lot of rattlesnakes on our expeditions. Neither of us was ever struck, even if we were much closer."

"What should we do?"

"Should we shoot it?" ask Samster. He knelt and from his backpack took out a small-caliber revolver.

Tully and Wendy recoiled. "What is *that*?" Wendy cried.

"It's the pistol my father left when he abandoned the family."

"You mean you've been hiking with a gun?"

Samster looked embarrassed. "Well, yeah. I didn't know what we'd find out here."

"So you brought a gawdammed gun?" said Tully.

"And why are you carrying a gun in your backpack?" demanded Wendy.

"In a word, Tony, but back to the rattlesnake, do we shoot it?"

"Absolutely not!" said Tully. "It doesn't pose any danger to us, and shooting it would just be gratuitous killing. Not to mention alerting anyone in the mountains that we're here, not that I think there's anyone else in the mountains. Still, you never know."

"I'm afraid of that snake," said Wendy, "but I'm terrified of that gun. What do you recommend, Tully?"

"I recommend we just leave the snake alone. It'll move on, and we won't see it again."

"What if it moves on to our campsite?" asked Wendy.

"That's pretty unlikely, but when we return we can do a thorough search using our walking poles to make sure no other snakes are in the area. And we'll put all our gear in our tents."

As they talked the snake stopped rattling and cautiously began sliding away.

"Now let's resume what we were doing, but away from the snake," said Tully, "and in the meantime, Samster, put that damned gun away."

Sheepishly Samster knelt to put it back in his backpack.

#

They built a small fire at their campsite. A search of its vicinity had revealed nothing dangerous. As they sat sipping herbal tea that would not keep them awake, Wendy turned to Samster.

"So, about the gun? ..."

"I'd like to see it," said Tully. Wendy cringed when Samster took it from his pack. They looked at Samster. "Is it loaded?" asked Wendy.

"I think so."

"You *think* so!" she squealed. "You don't know? I think I'll go hang out with that rattlesnake, at least it knows it's loaded."

Tully took pity on his friend. "I'll tell you what. I'll unload the gun—if it's loaded—then I'll carry the bullets and Samster you carry the gun. Wendy, does that make you feel better?"

"A little. How about we just leave the gun here and retrieve it on our way out. Or better still, don't retrieve it. But then I don't expect you two to agree to something as sensible as that, so I'll settle for keeping the gun and the bullets separate."

Samster was embarrassed and angry. Once again he'd cast himself in the role of fool. He'd had to admit he didn't know how to use the gun, didn't even know if it was loaded. Tully determined that it was loaded.

But neither Wendy nor Tully had had family members roughed up by Tony. Wendy losing her job, which she appeared happy to lose. Tully facing problems with his dissertation committee. But he and his mother and brother were facing physical violence from an armed, violent psychotic thug with a history of physical aggression.

#

As the fire died down each sat in private thought beneath the moonless sky. Wendy listened for the sound of hissing and slithering and rattling in the dark silence.

And when she heard nothing she thought about Samster and his predicament. Good old Samster. Along with Tully he'd been the only one ever to take her photography seriously—but had she ever taken him seriously? He was always just there, the happy, wacky stoner, good for a laugh. The essential good-times ingredient in all their get-togethers. Howdy's defender, because they were so much alike.

What could she do? For the first time her practicality and commonsense failed her.

Good old Samster. Poor old Samster. She wiped a tear from her eye.

#

Tully also thought of Samster. He too had no idea what to do. He had underestimated Tony's threat to him and his family. And the gold obsession resulted from Samster's desire to help his family.

That was Samster. Always there to help, in his slap-happy way, offering a ride to school, acting as a go-between with Wendy, fixing his bicycle, or having Elron fix his computer.

What had he done for Samster? Sure, he'd always been a good friend, but that hadn't been very demanding. Now he felt completely inadequate.

What if they found the mine tomorrow? What if there really was gold to be had? He knew that Samster had been far more eager for the gold than he was; now he knew why.

He'd happily give his share of the treasure to Samster, if it would help him.

Tully scoffed at himself. There he was again, living in a fantasy world. "His share of the treasure—" as if there would be any treasure, as if there had ever been any treasure. He didn't know what they'd find tomorrow, but he was certain it wouldn't be a shaft filled with glittering rocks.

And his disappointment wouldn't approach Samster's. No, he'd go back to his research; maybe move on to another treasure hunt, though he couldn't imagine one to equal this one. But Samster would be crushed. And he'd been the one who'd infected his friend with this untreatable virus; even as Tully was debunking the treasure tales to Samster he nonetheless was reveling in their allure and romance.

It was he who had summoned Crazy Tony, like an evil demon, into their lives, like the sorcerer's apprentice uttering spells he couldn't understand or control.

He'd even lost Wendy to the fools-gold fantasies.

Tomorrow they'd know. They'd find the mine—or they wouldn't. He knew the best thing would be to pack up in the morning and head home, but it was too late for that. They had to follow this hostile, tortuous canyon in the Sierra del Sombre wherever it led.

CHAPTER 26

During the night lightning had flashed overhead, and they heard raindrops on their tents. They spent most of the rest of the night listening for the roar of a flashflood.

"It looks like we dodged the bullet," said Tully as he emerged from his tent to a clear blue sky.

"I think it was karma," said Wendy from inside the tent. "I think not shooting that rattlesnake saved us. Now do me a favor and scan the area thoroughly for rattlesnakes," she said as he stood in the pre-dawn chill. "I'm not leaving this tent until you do."

He shrugged.

As daylight crept down the canyon, Tully surveyed the campsite, probing beneath rocks and bushes with his walking pole. As expected he didn't find any snakes; you never find them when you're looking for them.

He listened. Utter silence. He sniffed the air. Completely empty of smells save for a vague background scent of distant rain.

"All clear," he announced. With that Wendy and Samster emerged. Using a tiny camp stove he made coffee; breakfast would be cold granola.

With the maps spread before them, Tully said, "As near as I can tell, if this really is the right canyon, the spot marked Oro should be three canyon turns away. I've marked it on the topographic map, but keeping track of canyon turns is difficult, so we'll have to be watchful."

They packed up, then descended to resume hiking in the canyon's bottom. "Look at the rocks here," Tully said. "If there was a mine here, some of the rocks would have washed down. They wouldn't have had gold in them, like Samster's rock, but they'd be the same stuff, and they'd be angular, not smooth and water-tumbled.

"And look for any signs of human activity—an old trail, debris, anything."

They moved slowly. Samster was quickest to spot anomalous rocks, but none bore a resemblance to the sample in his backpack.

They marked the first bend in the canyon. "Should be just a couple more," Tully said.

#

They had hiked a quarter-mile farther when they came to the second bend. Suddenly Wendy said, "Here's something, but I'm afraid it's not what we were hoping for."

Tully and Samster rushed forward. Across the canyon was stretched a stout barbed-wire fence. On it was a sign reading: "White Sands Missile Range. Entry prohibited. Violators will be subject to arrest and prosecution. Area potentially contaminated with explosive devices. Do not disturb any items."

"Shit!" said Tully. "I was afraid of this."

"What do you mean?" asked Samster.

"If you look closely at the topo map, you can see the boundary lines of the Missile Range, and they go through here. I was hoping the boundary wouldn't be marked on the ground."

"What now?" asked Samster.

Tully just shook his head. "I don't know. According to the map, the Oro is just around the next bend, probably only a hundred yards, or less. We're so close."

"We could get in and get out before anyone knew we were there," said Samster.

"Are you *insane*?!" shouted Wendy. "Samster, you sound like a house burglar. I can't believe you two are actually standing here talking about breaking into a highly guarded, top-secret military facility. They have surveillance equipment that can detect and analyze a coyote fart from ten miles away. And for what? What will you tell them as they prepare to haul your stupid asses off to jail? Will you tell them you were just looking for a lost gold mine? Might as well, it'll give you a shot at an insanity plea."

She looked at Tully in desperation. His face contorted with indecision. "Tully?" Wendy squeaked.

Samster just stared at him.

Finally Tully said, "Wendy's right: What we have to lose if we're caught overwhelms what little we have to gain if we succeed. God! It hurts to say this. We've come so far, we're so close. But the chances of finding Toler's gold mine are, well, just plain minuscule. And what if, against all odds, we find it? Unless the gold is in big chunks, which it almost never is, we can't take it out or work the claim, or even go back at night without eventually getting caught."

Turning to Samster, who appeared stricken. "Please, consider. Recklessness here can mess up our whole lives. We should walk away. I'll probably wonder the rest of my life what we'd have found up in the canyon, just around the next bend, and maybe someday, in a way I can't foresee, I will know. But I'm not going to ruin my life or the lives of people I love." He took Wendy's hand.

They looked at Samster, whose eyes were wild with desperation. "Maybe finding the lost mine doesn't mean that much to you, but to me it's a chance at a better life for me and my family. All my life I've just been content to be a slacker and a loser—and I'm tired of it. This my big chance to go for something more than being just a part-time wrench at a bike shop. Besides, we've got the map. Are we just going to forget about the map, make like it never existed?"

Suddenly a harsh voice. "I'll take care of the map. In fact, I'll solve the whole problem for you."

They spun around. "Tony!" Tully cried.

"Yeah, it's Crazy Tony," he smirked. "You think I don't know what you call me? But I wasn't too crazy to track you down, and now I'll take the map and see for myself what's up in the canyon. Hand it over."

"It's on White Sands Missile Range," said Wendy.

Tony grunted a mirthless laugh. "I know that. No strand of barbed wire and a sign ever kept me from going where I wanted to go. Now let's have the map."

"Samster, give it to him," implored Wendy. Samster looked at Tully, who nodded.

Slowly Samster knelt and with shaking hands he reached into his backpack. When he took them out they held the gun.

"Samster!" Wendy screamed.

"I've been a passive loser all my life—but no more. I found this map, not her, not him," he said nodding to Wendy and Tully. "It's mine. I'm not giving it up."

Tony's eyes widened, then narrowed. "That's a cute little gun. I'll bet your daddy gave it to you for your sixth birthday. But judging from the looks of the cylinder, he didn't give you any bullets."

Samster hesitated, then said, "It's got one bullet in the chamber, that's all I need."

"Yeah, if it's there. Now, speaking of guns, *this* is a *real* gun." And before Samster could react he pulled aside his jacket and from a holster withdrew an enormous pistol and pointed it at Samster. "Yep, *this* is a gun, a .357 magnum, to be exact, and before you could pull the trigger on your little toy it would blow a hole in you big enough to drive a train through. Now put that thing down before someone gets hurt."

"Samster!" Wendy screamed, "do what he says."

"Wendy's right," Tully said.

Samster knew he had no choice. Tony had called his pathetic bluff, and he was left holding a little empty gun. Kind of the story of his life, he thought. If it wasn't for Wendy and Tully, he'd have been tempted to tell Tony to go ahead and shoot.

Then suddenly he whipped his gun arm around and with his empty gun struck Tony's hand, knocking his pistol onto the sand. As Tony scrambled for his gun Samster yelled "Run, run!" to Wendy and Tully as he ran to the fence. In one motion he vaulted over it and dashed up the canyon. "I know where the mine is, but it's mine, rightfully mine. No one is taking it from me. I'm going for it."

Tully grabbed Wendy's arm and began running down the canyon. Holding his gun, Tony glanced at them then began running up the canyon after Samster. Awkwardly he swung his legs over the fence and yelled, "You stop right now and give me the map or you'll wish you had," but Samster already was out of sight. Clumsily Tony began running after Samster.

#

Tully and Wendy ran headlong down the canyon. Finally, out of breath, they paused where the side canyon joined the main one. "Shouldn't we go help Samster?" panted Wendy.

"We'd only make things worse. We should do what Samster said," Tully answered. "We run, get out of these damned mountains and go for help."

Wendy hesitated only a second before nodding. They resumed trotting down the canyon.

Suddenly they heard a gunshot behind them.

Tully stopped, staggered, as if shot himself. "Samster!" he screamed. "Samster!" Nothing. He sank to his knees in the sand.

Wendy stared at him wide-eyed. He rose, then began lurching back up the canyon.

"No," said Wendy, grabbing his shoulder. "We don't know what's happening back there—and maybe you'll get shot yourself. We should do what Samster told us to do: run, and get help."

Alternately walking and trotting, they made their way down the canyon they'd hiked up the day before.

The sun was declining when finally they made it to the canyon's mouth. Exhausted and still terrified, they sat on a rock. In the distance they could see the windmill beside which was their car.

Suddenly from behind them, "You beat me, but not by much."

They wheeled around. "Samster!"

Striding down the canyon was their friend. "I'm glad that for once someone did what I recommended," he said smiling.

"We heard a shot," said Wendy.

"Tony was having trouble keeping up with me, so in a straight stretch of the canyon, where he could still see me, he got off a shot. It just missed me, hit a rock outcrop, spattered me with rock fragments."

"Oh, Samster," Wendy moaned.

"It was perfect," said Samster. Wendy and Tully looked puzzled.

"It convinced me I couldn't argue or negotiate with Tony. So in the canyon's twists when he couldn't see me, I yelled at him, 'You can have the map. I put it under a rock in the center of an X I made in the sand. Just leave us alone. The map and the mine are all yours.'

"Then I scampered up an arroyo. I knew he wouldn't follow, at least immediately, he'd be too busy looking for the map and then examining it. I went cross-country and made it back to the main canyon—and here I am."

"So you gave him the map?" asked Tully.

"I did. That was the whole point of what I did, it wasn't to protect the map, it was to protect you. And it worked."

Tully and Wendy could only stare. Finally Tully said, "Not bad, for a loser-slacker."

#

They jogged-marched back to their car, where they also found Tony's pickup.

"Should we disable it?" asked Wendy. "Deflate the tires, drain the radiator?"

"No," said Tully. "That would only infuriate him. Right now he's got what he came for, the mine. And we might have got what we came for, to be rid of him. He's got no reason to come after us anymore. Let's leave it at that. True, we lost the mine, but maybe not. I'll explain as we drive back."

#

They drove toward Socorro as fast as Wendy's Honda would go, Samster constantly looking behind them for Tony's pickup. Finally, as they approached the city's outskirts, they relaxed.

"Okay," said Samster to Tully, "What's this about not necessarily losing the mine. Seems to me that between homicidal Crazy Tony and the Missile Range it's pretty much out of our reach."

"Okay," said Tully, "here goes. First, the map says *Oro*, but it doesn't say *mina* or *mine*. I don't have a clue as to why Toler wrote that on the map, but I'm skeptical the mine is in the Sierra del Sombre."

"And why is that?" asked Wendy.

"We know that the gold-bearing rock Samster found is dacite, and we know the Sierra del Sombre has dacite formations. But dacite like all minerals takes different forms, flavors if you will, based upon subtle differences in chemical composition.

"As we were hiking in the Sierra del Sombre I saw lots of dacite rocks, but none of the them matched the dacite in

Samster's rock. Samster's rock looked almost as out-of-place in the Sierra del Sombre as in the Chupaderas.

"Tony never saw Samster's rock, he just knows we were searching for dacite, so he'll spend his time examining all the dacite outcrops in the vicinity of the *Oro*—and I don't think he'll find anything."

"I'd sure like to believe that," said Samster.

"So what do we do now?" asked Wendy.

"What we should have done in the beginning. Show that rock to someone at the Bureau of Geology and get solid information. That's where we should go now."

#

They sat in the office of Bruce Overbee, mining historian at the N.M. Bureau of Geology in Socorro. Bookshelves lined the walls, but instead of books they held mining artifacts: headlamps, miners' helmets, single-jack drills, iron hammers, retorts, and scales. All the books in the office were piled on the floor. Yet rather than being a crusty old miner type Overbee was a trim, thirty-something man with short dark hair dressed in tan slacks and a blue denim shirt.

Tully, Samster, and Wendy sat in front of Overbee's large, cluttered desk, in the center of which was Samster's rock. They had told him of finding the map, then following the geology library lead to Lester Toler and the prospect pit in the Chupadera Mountains. "We deduced that the dacite rock hadn't come from the Chupaderas," Samster said, "so we did more detective work and concluded the map depicted the Sierra del Sombre, which does have dacite.

"We went there to find the mine, but, well, it's a long story, but we got wrong with a local guy named Tony Kalvari ..."

Overbee interrupted. "Oh, no. Tony Kalvari? I wish we could have warned you. Everyone at the Bureau knows him, or about him. He's a local treasure hunter—there are a lot of them—but unlike most he's not just a harmless hobbyist. He's mean, and dangerous, and crazy."

"We call him Crazy Tony," said Wendy. Overbee just nodded.

Tully continued the story. "Tony found out about the rock and started following us and threatening us. We decided the way to get rid of him was to find the mine, but Tony followed us into the Sierra del Sombre. That's likely where he is as we speak, trying to use the map to find the mine."

"He shot at Samster," Wendy said.

"I used the map to get him away from us. I have plenty of copies of the map, and anyway the supposed mine is on the White Sands Missile Range."

"The thing is," Tully continued, "when we actually got into the Sierra del Sombre and compared the dacite there with the dacite in the rock Samster found, they didn't match, so now we suspect the rock didn't come from the Sierra del Sombre at all."

Overbee picked up Samster's rock and examined it closely. Then he said, "Come with me."

They followed him down a hall in the Bureau of Geology building to a large room labeled Museum. He led them to a glass case and pointed to a rock labeled "Gold ore, White Raven Mine, White Oaks Mining District."

The rock matched Samster's rock.

"The White Raven Mine was an important producer back in the 1880s," Overbee explained. "It shipped a lot of ore, hired almost fifty miners. They were high-grading the ore like crazy, despite everything the mine's owners did to stop them, samples of the White Raven's ore were all over southern New Mexico. That was how we got this sample, an old miner left his rock collection to the Bureau.

"You say you found this in a prospect pit in the Chupaderas? My guess is that a White Raven miner needed a place to stash his stolen ore. That's how much high-grading was going on, the miners created caches that they could return to and get gold when they needed it."

"Might one of the miners have created a cache in the Sierra del Sombre?" asked Tully.

"Sure. Actually, the Sierra del Sombre would have been a good place for a cache, as it's about half-way between the White Raven and Socorro, which was the center for mining activity at the time. Close—but not too close. Better than the Chupaderas, which had too many prospectors crawling over them."

"So Tony is not going to find a gold mine in the Sierra del Sombre?" asked Samster.

"No, if he's lucky, he'll find a few gold-bearing ore samples—or not. Toler might have removed them. A wild goose chase. Probably the story of Tony's life."

CHAPTER 27

"Tully, I have something to tell you that could be either good or bad for you, depending upon what you do with it," said Elnora as Tully settled into the chair in front of her office desk.

Tully arched his eyebrows. He didn't like the sound of this. He hadn't spoken with Elnora since the Sierra del Sombre expedition. He knew he should tell her about it, but it would mean he'd gone treasure-hunting instead of working on his dissertation. He doubted he could explain the mitigating circumstances to her.

"Things here in the department are going from bad to worse. I won't burden you with the details, except to say that Spencer has been obsessed with remaking the department to his vainglorious liking. Eventually he will overreach and suffer a fall, but in the meantime I don't have the energy or the backing to oppose him.

"I have a friend, a former fellow graduate student, who's now a dean at a small college in Colorado, Summit College. Ever hear of it?"

Tully shook his head. "Can't say that I have."

"No one has. It's not exactly Harvard, or even the University of New Mexico. In fact, it would be a stretch to call it the University of Summit County. It gets almost no grants, has a tiny student body, but it does have several generous and loyal alumni. Its faculty rarely are published in academic journals, though when they are they tend to get noticed, and the salaries are abominable."

"Let me guess: you're going there."

"Good deduction, Tully."

"It's gotten that bad here?"

"It has, but that's not the only reason. Actually, some of it has to do with you."

Again Tully arched his eyebrows.

"I've made many compromises in my career, and many of them are the same ones I've asked you to make. Now, don't get me wrong: I still think you need to sacrifice your passion for lost treasures to finish your dissertation, just as I dropped many interests to finish mine. It was the right decision for me, and it will be for you—if you make it.

"But compromises are like shortcuts on the path of life, and if you take too many you risk losing the path altogether. I've come close to doing that. Fortunately, if you don't let your original vision die, and if you look for opportunities to keep it alive, they will appear."

Tully leaned forward, his elbows on her desk, staring intently at Elnora.

"As they have with Summit College. I never expected to make a big splash in the history field, and I haven't. But I do have historical interests that I am passionate about what I've put aside.

"Summit College is in the central Colorado Mountains. I'll be able to track down the truth of Hardrock Molly. I'll probably write a book about it that could sell modestly. I'll probably encounter other mysteries that will tug at me. Maybe I'll supplement my meager salary by working part-time in a bookstore, as other faculty members do. I hate to leave my beloved home, but I'll find another place to love—and my cats will transplant well. I'm very excited, an emotion I haven't felt for a long time."

A broad grin spread over Tully's face. Impulsively he extended his hand and shook Elnora's, then, embarrassed, leaned back.

She paused, then continued. "Thank you, Tully. It's typical of you that your first reaction was happiness for me, not concern for yourself."

Tully's face reddened, his grin faded.

Elnora continued. "Don't worry, I'm not going to throw you overboard; this move won't happen overnight. I'll still be here to help you through the department's shark-infested waters, but as I told you the last time we spoke, there's no time for distractions. Set a timer on how much time you spend eating. Live like a monk. No more treasure-hunting."

Tully shifted uneasily in his seat. "Uh, a lot has happened since we spoke." She frowned. He told her about the expedition to the Sierra del Sombre, omitting nothing. "There is no Lost Oro Mine, but I had to search for it to learn that."

She shook her head, overwhelmed. "Does that mean Crazy Tony won't be a threat anymore?"

"Crazy Tony won't be threatening anyone for a long time. When Tony followed Samster up the Sierra del Sombre canyon onto White Sands Missile Range property, he was picked up almost immediately by Range security cameras. Then he made the colossal but predictable mistake of shooting at guards when they came to evict him. He actually thought he'd found the mine. Given his record, he'll be incarcerated for a long time. So, no, neither he nor the mine will be distracting me."

"I'll bet Wendy's relieved."

"Actually, she's one reason I'll be focused on the dissertation. In the Sierra del Sombre I finally realized that our future together was worth more than any lost treasure, real or imagined."

Elnora started to say something, but Tully interrupted her. "She's undergoing a career change too. She wants to become a photographer. She showed her Bean Country photos to a gallery in town. They liked them and want to give her an exhibition. Her images are truly professional, she just needs recognition. And part of the deal is that I write catalog copy for the exhibition. It's just a few months away. That means I have to finish my research by then.

"Wendy will be busy too. She's starting a new job, at a Starbucks. The pay is significantly less than she was making at the preschool, but at least she won't be dealing with tantrums from parents and children. At least I think she won't."

Elnora smiled and shook her head. "Life is strange. I wonder if she'd be interested in Hardrock Molly sometime."

"I know she would. The Southwest has lots of photographers, but not many are married to historians, so capturing and interpreting history is her orientation."

"Tully, you've reaffirmed my faith in the future, which is a good quality for an historian."

"Actually," Tully said, "there is one mystery I'll be pursuing." He told her about Eduardo Duran.

"I can't forget his face, staring at me from the old photo in the state archives. It haunts me, especially that no one knows what happened to him. And Samster can't forget about him either. Sometimes when I look at that photo I see shadows of Samster; he might be a relative. But don't worry, I won't let that derail the dissertation, but I won't forget about him either."

Elnora laughed. "Good! That's just what you should do. And for all we know, you and I will jointly discover that somewhere in the maze of the past Eduardo Duran met Hardrock Molly, and they ran away to California together."

#

Wendy was waiting for Tully when he got home.

"Well?" she asked. "Did you tell her about the Sierra del Sombre? And how did she take it?"

"She had news of her own," said Tully. "You call Samster while I order a pizza. We have things to celebrate."

"Why are you in such a good mood? And I'll bet poor Samster doesn't have anything to celebrate."

Tully frowned. "True, but let's do it anyway."

The pizza and Samster arrived simultaneously at the apartment. Wendy turned to Samster and said, "Grinning Tully here apparently had a good afternoon and wants to tell us about it and celebrate."

"Great," said Samster, "because I also had a good afternoon."

They looked at him with surprise. Finally Tully said, "You go first. You've needed a good afternoon more than I have."

Wendy distributed pizza on paper plates as Samster began.

"The Sierra del Sombre was the best thing that's happened to me. It was the first time I took control and made things happen, instead of letting them happen to me. It was worth having Tony shoot at me."

"So what happened that made today a good day?" asked Wendy.

"The news is that you two will have to get along without Samster for a couple of years. That is, unless you're willing to visit me in El Salvador."

"What?"

"You're running away to Central America?" asked Wendy.

"Not running away, running toward. I've been talking to a Peace Corps recruiter. I can't teach English or build a bridge or organize a community—but I can repair bicycles. And bicycles are how many people in rural El Salvador get around.

"Sure, they know how to kluge together a broken bike and get it rolling, but that's not the same as actually knowing how to fix them, make them solid and serviceable. I can do that. But more importantly, I can train them to do that.

"It took fast talking to get them to agree that having good hands with a spoke wrench was more important than a college degree. I'll be going for in-country training in two weeks.

"While I'm gone, Mom can rent my room for enough money to pay for fixing up the other room. And I'll be able to send money home."

"Samster!" Wendy said. "That's brilliant."

"It is, dude," said Tully.

Then Wendy's face darkened with concern. "But El Salvador is a violent country."

"That's why I get to go there. Not many people are willing to go. If I'd said I wanted to go to Thailand or Nepal, I don't think the Peace Corps would have been interested in me, given my educational and employment background. But when I said I wanted to go to rural El Salvador they took another look."

"Oh, Samster," said Wendy. "I'm afraid for you. I think it's a great idea, leaving the country and all, but El Salvador ..."

"I'm afraid too. But they were happy when I said I wanted to be posted to the most remote, undeveloped part of the country. El Salvador deserves a second chance, and so do I. We're a perfect match. Besides, I'm Hispanic and speak Spanish."

Tully beamed at him, then said mischievously, "But wait, before you go shouldn't we go back to Arizona and find the Lost Dutchman Mine? With its gold we won't have to become a monk in the library, sling coffee, or repair bikes in El Salvador. Come on, whattaya say?"

He almost dodged the pizza boxes.

Then Samster reached into his backpack and took the gold-flecked sample he and Tully had found. He gave it to Wendy. "Here, keep this while I'm gone. I know it's safe with you."

Then Tully said to Wendy, "I have something for you too." He reached into his pocket and pulled out the little vial containing the gold he'd found panning on the Rio Grande. "I still want you to have this. It's safer with you than with me."

263

She took it, kissed him, then laughed, "Just as long as Samster's rock and this are the only gold in your life. And for a wedding ring, I think I'd prefer an agate amulet in the shape of a bean."

THE END

ALSO BY ROBERT JULYAN

The Place Names of New Mexico, the indispensable standard reference for the named geographical features in New Mexico.

Sweeney, winner of the 2012 Tony Hillerman Fiction Award of the New Mexico-Arizona Book Association.

The Mountains of New Mexico, the natural and human history of all the mountains in New Mexico.

Hiking to History, the stories behind New Mexico historic sites that can only be reached by hiking.

New Mexico's Wilderness Areas; the complete guide, produced in cooperation with the New Mexico Wilderness Alliance, this is the definitive guide to New Mexico's wildernesses, study areas, and wild lands.

The Field Guide to the Sandia Mountains, co-editor and contributor, deals with only one area, the Sandia Mountains east of Albuquerque, but it includes *everything* one would want to know about these mountains within 50 miles of half of the state's population.

Beobuck, a delightful children's fantasy about a giant bear and those who loved him.

Best Hikes with Children in New Mexico, a statewide selection of hikes focused on adventures and features that will appeal to children as well as adults.